More by the Author

Horror

Dissonance Junction

From the Shadows

The Dark Collective

Granny Bael

Anthologies

Unnerving: Volumes 1—3

The Mighty Pen

Tales of the Slug

Lauren Patzer

BLUE FORGE PRESS
Port Orchard, Washington

To the abused, oppressed, and downtrodden—I see you, I hear you and, to some extent, I have been you. Never give up! There are solutions and allies around every corner, just as much as there are enemies that sometimes come from unexpected places.

GRANNY BAEL

Lauren Patzer

1

RIVER WALK

Jemma stared at the surface of the river as it flowed slowly along its inexorable path. Her mother's words when she got home earlier that day still echoed through her mind.

"No one can protect you from the shit life throws at you," Diedre Dawkins slurred through her drunkenness as she lay on the couch. She brushed black hair out of her eyes and tried to focus bloodshot dark eyes on her eldest. "Surely not your loser father…."

Jemma felt the irony of the words strike at her heart. Her mother's life didn't start out easy and while she had made strides, most of her life had never been under her control. Diedre's smooth olive complexion was exotic enough to get her out of the Chinese orphanage and into the mail order bride business—a mixed blessing at best. Her upbringing in an orphanage stuffed with other unwanted female children would have been mired in poverty. Her advancement to being groomed as a mail order bride meant food and education, but a life of strict rules and restrictions ultimately resulting in a continued life of servitude to the whim of others. Diedre, of course, wasn't her given name but the one assigned to her under a marketing research decision for the American market. She was so young when she began her training regimen, she didn't remember her original name.

The resulting arranged marriage was at her grandfather's direction, Jemma had learned, after a few drunken tirades between Diedre and Jemma's father, Lawrence. Her grandfather, Elbert Dawkins, insisted on the coupling and, given his control over his son, he always got what he wanted. Elbert theorized a cultured, trained wife was just the thing that Lawrence needed to make up for his shortcomings, or at least that's what he loved to say of his eldest son whenever given the opportunity. Jemma never learned exactly what those shortcomings her grandfather referred to were, but a short temper was likely one of them.

Her parents first few years together were relatively blissful. Diedre was the doting wife and acclimated to American life fairly quickly. Jemma vaguely recalled pleasant childhood memories of her mother and even her father. It took several years before the tensions reached the surface. Jemma never knew what her mother went through in China but something dark seemed to have surfaced. Combined with her father's own brutal upbringing, it was only a matter of time before the two dysfunctional adults clashed.

Her father walked through the door and started screaming at her mother. "Dammit, Diedre! Can't you lay off the bottle for a fucking second?"

Jemma slowly backed away from the ensuing argument. The familiar refrain of her father being weak and her mother being trapped were enough to make her ill. Diedre had no family to fall back to in China, only a contract signed and paid for years ago. That was enough to make anyone feel trapped. Even then, she thought her mother's condition might be somewhat postpartum as the drinking started soon after her younger brother was born. They'd had to switch him to formula because her mother's milk was tainted with alcohol. It was a great form of birth control, though; Jemma never wanted to have children. It also appeared likely she'd never have any more siblings. Her parents no longer slept in the same bed.

They used to be happier. Even though they were thrust together against their will, Jemma remembered a time when they truly cared for each other. She couldn't understand how that kind of love could just get lost.

A return to nature gave Jemma the measure of calm she needed to process her parents' volatility. The river always calmed her; its resilience was so unlike human emotion. The soothing, rhythmic sound of the flowing water punctuated by the occasional bird shrilling in the trees took her away from her life if only for just a few moments.

She hefted the flat rock in her hand and sent it flying across the surface of the river, skipping it four times. Jemma grinned.

"How do you get it to skip so many times?" a voice asked behind her. Jemma gasped and twirled around. Teek flashed his typical mischievous smile. He was always getting the jump on his friends. His olive skin and slightly oval eyes mirrored her own, betraying their shared Asian heritage even if they weren't exactly related.

"Fuck, Teek! Why are you always scaring people?" she hollered and punched his arm firmly.

"Ow!" Teek whimpered overdramatically. Behind him, Jemma's other friends Dom and Mary laughed.

"Oh, you two were in on it?" Jemma scowled at them. Dom held up his hands in surrender.

"Nobody jumps like you do," he said, flashing his own bright smile that melted her heart instantly. She smiled even as she wondered if her attraction to his dark-skinned Adonis-like qualities were more admiration or more revenge at her parents for the relationship she wanted with him. They'd been friends since elementary, the four of them, brought together by family trauma and mutual outcast vibes at school. They stuck together and pushed the bullying ways of the other kids aside for the most part.

"Come, on, Jem," Mary said as she descended deftly around the rocks. "What's your rock skipping secret? Or is it too juicy to share?"

"Okay, Mare," Jemma said as she bent down to pick up another projectile. "You need to start with a super flat rock that should fit in the palm of your hand like this." Jemma held up the rock for her gathered posse to see. "Then, you crook your inside finger around the rock and hurl it at the surface of the water with the same intensity you would your father's head." Jemma flung the rock across the water, but it only skipped three times this go round. She frowned.

"They were at it again, huh?" Dom asked. His smooth deep voice nearly made her forget her family troubles.

"Must be nice to have an imaginary family to hurl rocks at," Teek murmured.

"Teek," Dom growled.

"Sorry, Teek," Jemma said. "How're things at the puppy mill?"

"Same old, same old. They finally reported Danny missing. Three days they waited. I'm surprised they bothered—can't imagine how that will affect their monthly income."

"Cops say anything?" Mary said rubbing Teek's shoulders.

"Cops are worthless," Teek said and then looked sheepishly at Dom. "Sorry, Dom."

"Uncle Howard may be a good uncle," Dom said shaking his head. "But I don't think anyone in this town is a good cop."

Jemma threw another rock. This one plunked right in. "Bad angle, bad town," she said.

They spent a couple minutes skipping rocks, breathing in the cool afternoon air and just enjoyed the quiet company.

"Before it gets too late, I wanted to show you guys something I found yesterday," Teek said.

They all groaned.

"Teek," Mary said. "I don't think anybody is in the mood for day-old road kill."

"Gross," Jemma said.

"Naw, it's nothing like that," Teek said as he looked around quickly and then whispered, "I was poking around the District yesterday."

"Dude," Dom said. "It's condemned. You can't be poking

around those buildings. It's dangerous especially with the quakes."

"You gonna be a cop like your uncle?" Teek asked.

"The quarry is unstable and those warehouses are shambles just waiting to fall on people," Dom said.

"Good," Jemma said. Dom looked at her in shock. "Maybe some danger is just what we need to shake things up in this town."

Dom opened his mouth and then shut it. Jemma gave him a little smile, knowing he'd shut his mouth because he was sweet on her. Dom closed his eyes and shook his head.

"Cool, we're all in agreement!" Teek said and headed up the bank towards the road a couple hundred feet through the trees.

Dom looked at both of the girls and shook his head. He turned and rushed up the bank after Teek.

"Dude!" he shouted. "We're not going in any condemned buildings!"

Mary and Jemma made their way up the river bank at a more leisurely pace, taking care not to twist an ankle on the rocks.

"How's your mom doing?" Jemma asked.

Mary moaned a little and kept climbing.

"She has her good days and her bad days, but we all know how it's going to end. At least, we know how it's going to end for her," Mary replied as she navigated some driftwood.

"Sorry," Jemma said. "What about your dad?"

After they'd gotten to more stable ground, Mary looked at her and shook her head. "It's not any better. Dad's still being an asshole and his new bitch is just as bitchy as ever. They said when Mom passes I can go live with my aunt Abby," Mary said.

"I didn't know you had an aunt," Jemma said as she scrubbed river mud off her shoes onto some exposed tree roots.

"She's the psychic," Mary said quietly.

"Crazy Abby? She's your aunt?"

"She's not crazy, she's just eccentric."

"Well," Jemma said. "She's psychic, so she should be expecting you."

"Really, Jem? I expect that shit from Teek."

"Sorry," Jemma said. "Look at it this way—it'll be a shitload better than living with your dad and—"

"That bitch!" they finished in unison and laughed.

2
TALES

Teek marched up to an old shack halfway to the District, just on the edge of town. He climbed the worn stairs and approached the front door. The other three stopped just a few steps behind, not climbing onto the rickety porch.

"Teek," Dom whispered. "Why are we at Old Man Murphy's place?"

Teek turned around and just smiled at them. He reached over and knocked on the door while he watched their eyes. Old Man Murphy was the local bogeyman. Everyone in town shied away from him and it was rumored he ate any child that wandered onto his property at Halloween. It was superstition and maybe he created the tale himself to keep curious little monsters off his property, but the stigma was still very palpable.

The door swung open and an elderly man with a grizzled beard and scraggly gray hair peeked out at them.

"Teek?" the old man said gruffly. "What matter of ruffians

have you brought with you?"

"They're cool. I thought maybe you could give them some history lessons about Tuggville," Teek said.

The old man cackled.

"You want to hear scary stories again?" Old Man Murphy replied as he stroked his beard thoughtfully. "Alright, come in but mind the cat. He'll tear your fingers off while he's purring at you."

The kids entered the dusky room and were surprised to find fairly well kept furniture in a clean room. Old Man Murphy waved at the couch and took a seat in a recliner close by. The kids looked around with gaping mouths; all except Teek who'd been here before.

"Surprised?" Old Man Murphy asked. "I maintain the scary recluse façade to keep the undesirables out. But if Teek says you're good people, I believe him."

"Are you his grandpa or something?" Dom asked.

Old Man Murphy shook his head. "I helped Teek out once when he was getting undue attention from Able's gang back before they got put away. That was behind the grocery, wasn't it?"

Teek nodded. He didn't seem embarrassed by the story but rather had a genuine look of warmth in his eyes for Old Man Murphy. He might not be Teek's grandfather, but it seemed like he was the first and only adult to ever care about him. That kind of loyalty went a long way with a wayward youth like Teek.

"Murphy's about the only decent person I know in town, present company excepted," Teek said.

"Thanks for looking out for Teek, uh, Old Man Murphy," Mary said.

"Call me Murphy," he said as he waved his hand.

"Okay, Murphy," Mary said. She flipped her long blonde hair back over her shoulders and fixed her gaze on the old man. "What's in it for you?"

"Substitution," Murphy said firmly without hesitation. "You see, Kevin—that was Able's first name—was my grandson. Technically, he still is, but I digress. I didn't get anything but flack from the little brat since he was a toddler. He's a very troubled young man. I found out he'd robbed my house roughly a week before I caught him hassling Teek there in the alley. I put an end to that incident, but I knew there was no hope for Kevin. He'd always be a delinquent like his father. I told my daughter to stay away from that bum, but he had a truck and a big smile. That was enough for her, I guess."

"Tuggville doesn't seem to have a lot of happy stories," Jemma said.

"Well, I thought Teek was a decent kid. We got to talking and he's helped out around here more than I think I've helped him," Murphy smiled at Teek with genuine affection. "I couldn't ask for a better grandson, so I just kind of informally adopted him."

"Well, shit, you could do it formally," Dom said. "Sorry, I don't mean to be forward, but Teek's life at the puppy mill sucks."

"Puppy mill?" Murphy asked.

"Foster home," Teek said. "They just keep piling kids in there like sardines and collecting checks from the state. They treat us like shit, keep us all cramped up in dark rooms like a puppy mill whenever we're there. The older kids just try to be there as little as possible. I prefer to talk about things that aren't particularly shitty."

"Well," Murphy said. "That's fucking Tuggville for you; never take care of their own people. The town's cursed."

"That's what I brought them here to hear about—the curse of Tuggville," Teek said.

"Well," Murphy started, sitting back in his chair. "It's not a pretty tale. There's been a stain on this town for fifty years. Maybe that's why it's cursed to be as horrific as it is."

"I haven't heard about any curse," Dom said.

"Most families don't talk about it, especially the families that have been here since the beginning," Murphy said. He reached into his back pocket and pulled out a flask, taking a swig and coughing for a moment. The teens all looked at each other uncomfortably. Their families had all been stuck in this town for decades with the possible exception of Teek who knew very little about his deceased mother and nothing about his father.

"So, Murphy," Jemma said. "What's it all about?"

"You seem familiar," Murphy said. "What's your name?"

"Jemma," she replied. When Murphy raised his eyebrows, she continued. "Jemma Dawkins."

"Ah, one of the families at the center of the story," Murphy said.

"What?" Teek asked. "You didn't tell me anything about families being involved; you just said they burned a witch at the stake for something she might not have done."

"I gave you the watered down version for your entertainment, but if you're all going to hear it, you might as well hear it all as far as I know it anyway. Lord knows I'm one of the ones cursed by what happened," Murphy said and then took another swig. He was silent for a time and just seemed to stare off into nothing, his eyes focused on history and no longer in the present. "There was a small, but powerful family in town named Balsom in 1973. The town was suffering from the oil embargo sending gas prices skyrocketing and everyone was on edge. Neighbors snapped at each other over the smallest infractions. Jobs were getting scarce. Even the quarry was shut down for a while, the place most people in town worked. It was dark times for Tuggville, but it was about to get darker."

As he relayed the story, Murphy almost went into a trance traveling back in his memory to the start of the oil crisis and what came after. "The Balsoms were partners with the Dawkins at the quarry. They were rich and with that wealth came some eccentricities. The Dawkins were well acquainted with strange behavior themselves, but the matriarch of the Balsom family had them all beat. It was rumored she was into black magic, held séances, and put curses and spells on people. Surely there was some truth to the accusations, but people started to blame the Balsoms for everything that was happening—not just in town, but the whole country. Then, one day, they were all found murdered in their mansion. All were dead except Granny Balsom who lived on her own estate not far from the rest of the family."

He continued, "Everything in town was owned by either

the Balsom or the Dawkins families. So, it was a little strange when the rumor mill started that Granny Balsom had killed her family as part of a demonic ritual to consolidate all the wealth under her so she wouldn't have to share it with her offspring. That was all that was needed to start the mob that marched to her estate, dragged her out, and burned her alive at the stake right there. The mob outnumbered the police a thousand to one. There was little the police could do. The worst part is Elwin Dawkins was the one at the head of the mob egging them on, shouting 'burn the witch.' The crowd did as he instructed and before she died, Granny Balsom cursed the entire town for their treachery and murder. After that, they called her Granny Bael after the demon of the underworld. Fitting since she died in fire."

"Nobody told me about this," Jemma said. "Why are you trying to blame my family?"

"Nobody in your family told you and you'd be hard pressed to find someone in town who would. There isn't much in this town that happens without your grandfather's permission. Anyway, Elwin Dawkins inherited everything from the Balsom family under the partnership contract. He even lived in Granny Bael's estate, where your grandfather lives now. I'm sure you've been there."

Jemma looked down. She'd seen the foundation cornerstone on her grandfather's estate. It clearly said Balsom Manor, built in 1962. The timeline fit, but she couldn't believe her great-grandfather could be responsible for the horrific burning of Granny Bael.

"Okay, that sounds horrible, but so what? How does that

mean we're cursed?" Jemma said defiantly.

"Twenty-five years after her death, Granny Bael came back and wreaked havoc over all of Tuggville—including the death of your great-grandfather. He burned up in the town square. A small group of people banded together, lured her to the quarry, and defeated Granny Bael. But some say she still haunts the quarry, seeking out those who killed her family and defeated her."

"That's a great story," Dom said. "But it lacks a little punch. Not exactly a bogeyman-level scary story."

"Really?" Murphy said. "Dom or is that Dominic Tulley? Ask your Uncle Howard what happened to his brother, Edward. Of course, Mary over here would probably be a little more sympathetic knowing her aunt was also involved in hunting down Granny Bael."

"Geez, dude," Teek said. "That's not cool roping them into the tale like that. We just came to hear a scary story. Granny Bael burning children with fire when they misbehave—that was the story you told me!"

"Teek, you don't have a personal connection to the story. Your family wasn't involved in hunting Granny down, but the rest of your friends all have a connection. I thought they should know." Murphy took another swig from his flask.

"Drunken old man with boring stories," Jemma said. She looked at Teek. "Real nice."

Jemma stormed out and Dom followed her. Mary lingered a bit to give Teek a withering stare and then followed her friends out the door.

"Murphy," Teek said frowning at the old man. "You said it

yourself—Tuggville sucks." Teek stormed out of the house hoping to catch up with his friends.

Murphy's cat jumped up onto his lap. He petted it absently as he stared at the door. "Well, Sigmund. I wish I knew the whole story. Maybe they'll be able to find it out now that I've set them on the path. Probably shouldn't have lied to Teek, though."

The cat bit Murphy on the hand and he shouted out in pain. Sigmund ran out of the room. Murphy looked at his finger where the cat had broken the skin. He sucked on the wound for a moment.

"Stupid cat."

3

THE BARN

Teek walked far behind his friends. They'd made it pretty clear they were pissed. It wasn't the first time. He sighed.

He watched them peel off in the directions of their individual homes. Teek didn't head to his own. He traipsed through the woods to a forgotten field with a dilapidated barn sitting in the middle of it. He checked for anyone watching, but it was just as abandoned as a remote, abandoned farm should be. He stepped up to the creaky barn door and edged it aside to slip in. The door barely moved on its hinges anymore and too much pushing on it would result in a dust and wood splinter shower, so he was very gentle with his manipulations.

The inside of the barn actually housed a small shack that looked fairly new. It was a sturdy construction with four posts, minimal walls and a roof to protect anyone inside from the possible crumbling of the old building above. A few hay bales sat inside with some blankets draped over them. The bales had been adjusted and shaped to form rough furniture and Teek sat down on one of them.

He stared sullenly at the roof of the shack. This was one of the only places he felt safe in the world. He chuckled when he thought about the tenuous and temporary nature of his safe haven. But even in this safe haven, he was never safe from his own dark thoughts. He'd never known a home without horror. His foster parents—it was hard to even call them parents—seemed bent on making life as unpleasant as they could possibly get away with. He wasn't sure he'd make it to the end of high school before things got too bad for him to stay in Tuggville. He imagined life on the streets anywhere else in the world had to be better than this; but he couldn't be certain of that and so he still remained.

He wasn't sure how much time had passed before he heard someone else push through the barn door. He glanced at the door and saw Mary's blonde head flashing in and out of the shadows.

"Hey," Mary said as she sat down next to him carrying a backpack. Teek nodded his head at her bag.

"You going on a trip?" he asked.

"No, silly," she replied as she unzipped the backpack and rummaged around in it. "I brought you a little food."

"I don't need that," Teek mumbled even as his stomach growled in opposition to his statement.

"It's just a couple peanut butter sandwiches and some fruit," she said as she pulled the bagged sandwiches out and set them on the makeshift hay table in front of them. She set some apples next to them. "I thought we could have a picnic, if that's all right."

Teek looked at the food and closed his eyes. A single tear threatened to emerge from his eye and he quickly sniffled and wiped his eyes.

"Okay, sure," Teek replied.

Mary unwrapped one of the sandwiches and bit into it. Teek grabbed a sandwich and tore it open. He started to devour the sandwich greedily.

"Slow down, cowboy. You don't have to fight anyone for your food here," Mary said. Teek stopped mid chomp and looked at her.

"Sorry," he said around a half chewed mouthful.

"It's okay. Besides, I brought two more sandwiches," she said. She squeezed his forearm. "You could use the protein."

Teek made a short chuckle and worked a little more slowly on eating the sandwich. He got free lunches at school, but breakfast and dinner were usually in short supply at the foster home. He tried to forgo eating anything at home because it meant less for the younger kids. That usually meant lifting a candy bar or a sandwich from the grocery, but he tried to keep it on the down-low.

"I'm sorry about Murphy. He's always been a cool dude and I didn't expect him to slam you guys like that."

"Not a big deal," Mary said smiling. "We take our fair share of abuse in this town. Really, I think everyone does. Like Murphy said, 'fucking Tuggville.' I spent some time last summer at the library. He's not wrong, but the details are sketchy even in what's recorded there."

"You never told us about it," Teek said as he frowned.

"Not a lot that's fit for sharing. It's bad enough I have to remember it forever, why put you guys through it?"

Teek tore into one of the apples like a man possessed until Mary gently patted him on the leg. He slowed down when he saw nothing but care in her eyes—her beautiful blue eyes. He cleared his throat and quickly looked down at the apple. She gently punched his shoulder and they laughed. They both ate the apples together in quiet contemplation.

"I know I'm a little difficult sometimes," Teek said.

"A little?" Mary asked with a smirk.

"Sometimes, I feel like I'm an outcast even in our little group of outcasts," Teek said.

"I think we all feel that sometimes," Mary said. "But I don't think that way about you."

"Thanks, but I—" Teek looked at Mary and his heart started to race. The light caught her face in just the right way, illuminating it like an angel. Before he even knew what he was doing, he reached his hand up to touch her, but held back. "Can I?"

Mary nodded and Teek touched her cheek softly. He ran his fingers gently through her hair and behind the nape of her neck. She closed her eyes and sighed. Teek moved his lips close to hers and gently brushed them. He felt her hand tighten on his thigh and he hesitated. When her hand relaxed a little, he pushed forward and kissed her. They kissed each other softly and then a bit more passionately, intertwining their tongues, becoming one in the moment.

They both jumped back when they heard the barn door groan a bit. They looked over and saw Dom pushing his athletic build through the door with a little less ease than they could, causing a cascade of dust and a few splinters to fall from the ancient door frame.

"Hey Dom," Mary said as she set herself a little further apart from Teek. She squeezed Teek's thigh firmly and slid her hand off slowly. Teek smiled and grabbed another sandwich. He ate this one a little more slowly, but savoring the flavor with a little more thought as now it reminded him of the kiss he'd just shared with Mary.

Dom walked into the shack as he brushed off the dust and wood splinters. He gave them a nod and sat down across from them. "Sorry about that scene at Old Man Murphy's place," Dom said.

"It seems like we're all apologizing to each other," Mary said. "How's Jem?"

"Well, you know how she gets. Quick to temper and slow to cool down. She'll come around. She's knows her family is shitty just like the rest of us. Different shit for different folks, I guess," Dom answered with a shrug.

"That stuff about her family is true?" Teek asked.

Dom nodded, something flashing across his dark face, but he just answered, "My deadbeat dad told me all the stories about the family dynamics running around town, the history, the deception. He said he was sick of it and that's why he left town, I guess. I don't know, maybe he's just an asshole and was looking for an excuse to leave us high and dry." Dom grabbed one of the apples and bit into it. He looked at both of them after he bit into it sheepishly. "Sorry, I haven't been home for dinner yet."

"You're not exactly high and dry," Teek said. Mary smacked Teek on the thigh.

"Just because I have a so-called father figure in the house, doesn't mean it's worth the trade off," Dom said. "I think my mom just has a soft spot for assholes who like to control her kids' lives."

"Sorry, man," Teek said. "Hell, Murphy's the closest thing I have to family in this town and look how that's turning out."

"Well, one thing my deadbeat dad had right. We need to get out of Tuggville as soon as we can. It's definitely cursed as fuck," Dom chewed thoughtfully on the apple. He looked out at the setting sun between the broken boards in the barn wall. "It's getting dark. I better get home before stepdaddy has another shit fit for me being out late. Thanks for the snack."

Dom got up and left. They watched him go and chuckled a little as he pushed through the barn door with some difficulty.

"You need to get smaller!" Mary yelled at him.

"Funny!" Dom hollered back as he walked away from the building.

Mary looked at Teek and smiled. She looked down and stroked his thigh gently.

"I better get back too before Mom worries about me," Mary said.

Teek stroked her cheek gently. She leaned into his touch.

"Okay," Teek whispered. "I'll see you tomorrow."

Mary gave him a quick kiss on the lips and grabbed her backpack. She walked out the door.

Teek watched her go through the cracks in the walls. He

munched on the last remaining apple.

"Maybe Tuggville isn't all bad," he murmured.

4
HOME

Dom opened the back door carefully. The door creaked just a little, but he was pretty sure his stepfather, Marv, didn't hear it over the college football game playing in the front room. He closed the door quietly and walked toward the stairs that led up to his room. If he was lucky, he wouldn't have to interact with Marv at all.

"Dom, that you?" Marv called from the front room.

Damn.

"Yeah, just heading upstairs to do some homework," Dom lied. He was pretty sure schoolwork was one of only two things Marv would let him off for.

"Come in here a minute," Marv said and then burped. Dom rolled his eyes. If Marv was watching college football, that meant he was drinking beer—a lot of beer. The evening just got particularly shittier.

"Yes sir," Dom replied putting on the fake smile he had to wear when talking to Marv. He walked into the front room.

34 Granny Bael

Marv sat in a recliner with his feet up wearing some heavily worn slippers, overalls, and a torn white tank top shirt that was so stained it was darker than Marv's pasty white skin. He had a bowl of cheese puffs on his lap, six empty beer cans haphazardly arranged on the side table next to him along with a ceramic plate with enough ketchup on it that it looked like a crime scene. There was an empty spot on that plate, but Dom wasn't sure what Marv had been consuming. No one was allowed to touch Marv's food on that side of the refrigerator.

Dom had a full set of protein shakes and low carb, high protein snacks in the pantry. Marv seemed to think that was all Dom needed to eat to stay healthy and get large. Dom snuck food from wherever he could when Marv was passed out, which he often was. He never seemed sober enough to notice Dom pulled some of his prized food from his precious collection. The other side of the fridge was nearly always barren except for whatever protein items Marv felt Dom needed to be consuming.

"Sit down," Marv said as he pointed to the couch. Dom sighed. If he was going to be sitting that meant Marv had decided it was time for one of his football pep talks that always made Dom feel like crap. Dom sat down.

"Where's Mom?" Dom asked, even though he knew the answer.

"Working," Marv replied and belched again. He stopped talking to take a swig from a beer tucked into the chair next to him. "She treats me like a king. Too bad your rat bastard father couldn't see that, huh?"

"Yeah," Dom said. He clenched his jaw and cleared

his throat.

"She's thinking about picking up a third shift—we need a new TV," Marv said.

Dom glanced at the seventy-two inch ultra high definition television with a crisp picture showing Alabama playing someone. Dom didn't really care who. He knew Alabama was where Marv thought he should go.

"What's wrong with this one?" Dom asked.

"It's too small! They got eighty-four inch televisions out there now! Gotta see Crimson Tide larger than life!" Marv laughed and Dom cringed.

"Maybe if you got a job—" Dom started.

"Don't get smart with me, son! I'm the head of this household—I'll do what I damn well please!" Marv took another swig of his beer. "Your mom loves providing all this stuff for me. Makes her happy. You want your mom to be unhappy?"

"No sir," Dom replied. He sat back on the couch and stared at the television. "Maybe I should get a job?"

"A woman's place is providing for her men! You'll do well to learn that. You'll have plenty of opportunity to provide for us when you get that pro contract after Alabama."

Dom looked down at the floor. He'd provide all right. He'd provide a way out of Tuggville for his mom and leave this worthless piece of shit to rot in this chair.

"Is that all?" Dom asked.

"No, that's not all, ya stupid fuck! Ya think I don't have something important to say? Huh?" Marv leaned forward toward Dom, shouting and spitting at the same time.

Dom grimaced.

"No sir," Dom replied.

"You know, we provide food and shelter for you and you act like it's not fucking enough, Dom! You got no respect for your elders! Life ain't a fucking gift, son, ya hear me?"

Dom sighed. It was nice to know Deadbeat Stepdad didn't have anything new to add to the conversation that he hadn't already heard from his deadbeat biological dad.

"Yes sir."

"Now pay attention—I talked to your mom last week and she said she hadn't talked to you about girls yet," Marv said.

"Oh shit," Dom muttered. There were going to be some wonderful, new things added to Marv's conversations now. Dom knew this drunken asshole would forget he'd talked about this too and bring it up for who knew how long.

"Now, you been fucking any girls?"

"Shit, Marv," Dom blurted out. "No, I haven't been with a girl."

"Good. Your mom screwed up her life when she got pregnant with you," Marv said. "She got preggers way too early. She should've dumped your fucking dad, for one. She should've graduated high school for another."

Dom rolled his eyes. His mom had graduated high school and been halfway to a college degree when she got pregnant. It had forced her to stop college for a while, but she'd gone back and gotten a nursing degree. Marv's history rewrite was one for the books.

"I don't want you dating anyone until you get that pro contract, ya hear me?"

"What?" Dom asked. "You want me to stay single and not date until I sign a pro contract for football?"

"That's right, you gotta focus! You get that contract, then me and your mom should be getting a new house and cars. That's what you owe the people who raised you. A nice fat retirement account too, you got it?"

"I hear you," Dom said.

"Don't go knocking up no worthless girl and fucking everything up." Marv took another swig of his beer and then shook it. It was empty. "Get me another beer."

Dom sighed and got up from the couch. He walked into the kitchen and grabbed another beer for Marv from the fridge. The bottom shelf of the fridge had two twenty-four packs of beer stuffed in it with about ten missing. Dom grabbed the beer and walked it back to Marv. As he handed the can to him, Marv grabbed him with his free hand.

"You got needs? You feel like knocking some girl up? You go grab some Vaseline and work on your arm strength, understand?"

Dom pulled his hand away. "I understand what you're saying," Dom said, trying to hide his disgust at the conversation and failing miserably.

"Good," Marv said. "Now go away—I've already missed more downs than you're worth."

"Yeah," Dom replied and left the room. He shook his head as he walked up the stairs.

When he reached his room, he opened the door quickly and stepped inside. He closed the door and breathed a sigh of relief. Marv might holler for him from downstairs, but Dom could just ignore him. Marv was too lazy and drunk to make it up the stairs to make an issue of it. He'd probably forget Dom had ignored him in the first place. He might even go get his own beer, but a dozen was usually his limit and he was close to that. It didn't look like he'd eaten much, so maybe eleven would do the trick and he'd pass out. Regardless, Dom was free of him for the night.

He sat down on his bed and looked out at the purple sky growing darker by the moment. He closed his eyes and felt the same color weighing on his mind. Just a little while longer and he'd be out of this godforsaken town, out from under this pitiful excuse for a home. He fantasized switching places with Teek for a moment, but Teek wasn't big like Dom and that would probably put him in the sites of Marv's fists. Getting bigger had at least put a stop to the violence Marv had visited on Dom during his drunken ramblings. Like a true coward, Marv only visited his violence on people he didn't think could protect themselves. That was probably why his mom was rarely home; better out from under Marv's aggression than facing it head-on. He might be able to defend his mom, but he couldn't be here all the time.

He thought about the one time he'd called the cops. His Uncle Howard had shown up, but the sheriff had told him to go home. They wouldn't let him handle the case since he was family. He remembered watching it all from a closet. Sheriff asked if everything was all right and Marv had told him there wasn't anything to worry about. Marv told the cop his wife was tired and cranky after work and sleeping after a long shift. Brat kid, Dom, had acted up and Marv had words with him. Little punk had called the cops. He told the Sheriff not to worry; he'd make sure they were never called out here for nothing again. Sheriff thanked him for his cooperation and left without even trying to see Dom or his mom. That night, Marv beat him so bad he missed the next week of school. He never called the cops again. That was six years ago.

Dom took off his clothes and lay down on the bed. He tried to think of Jemma, but his thoughts drifted toward his father instead—another failed father figure in his life. Left town ten years ago and wouldn't come back. He didn't fight Mom on the divorce. Deadbeat asshole never responded to the child support payment requests. He just called up every once in a blue moon, demanded Dom and his mother get out of Tuggville and always when he was so drunk his words slurred.

That was the biggest mystery of it all. What kept Mom here in this dead end town? Was it the pay? Surely she could get a job at any hospital in the country. She certainly couldn't be thinking she needed to stay to keep Marv happy. But then, that was the kicker. She'd gone from one abusive relationship to another and couldn't seem to break the cycle. Could he get her out or would he have to leave her behind forever when he left?

Mary stepped into the living room and saw the lone lamp on in the corner. No one was in the room. She sat down on the couch and rested her head on the back, looking up at the ceiling. The stucco seemed to shimmer in the dim light and Mary's mind immediately saw it as cancer crawling across the surface, undulating and ominous. She closed her eyes and sat forward.

"Oh, hi Mary," a voice said quietly. Mary opened her eyes and looked up as the home care nurse, Consuela, entered the room.

"Hi Consuela, how's she doing?" Mary asked.

"She's sleeping comfortably. Today was a good day. She had hardly any pain medication." Consuela picked up her sweater from the back of one of the dining room chairs. "How are you?"

"Well, I don't have cancer yet," Mary said grimly.

"You know this isn't hereditary, right?" Consuela said. "It's from drinking the water. You're not drinking the tap water are you?"

"No," Mary replied. "Only bottled water."

"Well, there you go. You should be fine." Consuela smiled and nodded. "It looks like Gwen will be here tomorrow just to check in on things."

Consuela walked to the front door and turned back to Mary. "You're going to be fine, Mary," Consuela said.

"Thanks," Mary replied and gave Consuela a smile. The nurse walked out the door and shut it gently behind her.

Mary sighed and sat back against the couch. She blinked and the tears started to leak from the edges of her eyes. She grimaced and sat up quickly, wiping her eyes and sniffling. She got up and walked into the kitchen. After taking a big swig from a refrigerated water bottle, she felt better.

She walked down the short hallway off the front room to her mom's bedroom and peeked through the cracked door.

Moonlight illuminated the room and Mary watched her mom in quiet slumber on the bed. She seemed at peace. Every few seconds, her chest would gently rise and fall. Mary stood there for a long time just watching her mom sleep. Her mind was empty of any thoughts. She just absorbed the moment and held it in her heart.

Finally, she went off to bed. As she changed into a night gown, she looked down at her hands in the cool moonlight. The bluish tint gave her skin the appearance of dead flesh. She shuddered and climbed into bed. She tossed and turned for a while before she fell into a troubled sleep.

The dream came again. Mary walked through the darkly lit funeral home; fog covered the floor and she walked in a daze toward the coffin set up in the chapel. To her left and right, the tops of the pews jutted out of the fog like sharks on the prowl. Light flashed intermittently under the fog illuminating shadowy things moving under the surface.

Mary stepped up to the coffin and saw her mom laying there in black robes. Even though Mary had never seen her dressed that way, the dream was always the same. Her mom lay in the coffin and Mary stood by watching helplessly. A flicker of orange caught Mary's attention. She looked up and saw the cross on the back of the chapel burning. The flames licked up the back wall and spread to the ceiling quickly. Mary gasped in shock. This was new.

Mary backed up just as her mom sat up in the coffin and turned to her.

"Why didn't you save me, Mary?" her mother asked. Then she burst into flame, quickly burned to a cinder and collapsed into a pile of ashes that littered the coffin and floated down into the fog on the ground.

The fog glowed in orange, yellow and red hues as if lit by flames from below. Mary backed up further.

"Help us, Mary!" came cries from below the fog. It was the voices of Dom and Teek. Dark hands thrust up from the fog, caught fire, and the skin burned until it bubbled and the skin peeled off.

"Help us, Mary!" the cries repeated. Mary turned to run and saw Jemma standing at the exit to the chapel dressed in the same dark robes her mother had worn. When Jemma looked up, her eyes were black as night.

"Why didn't you save us, Mary?" Jemma shouted in a deep voice Mary didn't recognize. Jemma flew through the air at Mary and—

Mary jerked awake in her bedroom, covered in sweat. She ripped the covers off and got out of bed, her jammies sticking to her like a second skin.

"Fuck," Mary whispered. "Like I needed that nightmare to get worse. Thanks, subconscious."

The phone rang and Murphy cursed as he got up from his old rocking chair on the porch. He grumbled as he stormed into the living room. Sigmund jumped down from the couch as the screen door slammed shut, running in front of Murphy, nearly causing him to tumble over the cat.

"Honestly, Sigmund! You trying to get killed? Life's short enough as it is," Murphy hollered at the retreating feline. He walked the short distance to the phone next to his recliner and picked it up.

"This better be important! You interrupted a perfectly lovely moon rise!" Murphy shouted angrily into the phone.

"It's Wayne," the voice on the other end responded. Murphy went stock still as he nodded.

"Well, thanks for getting back to me, Wayne." Murphy's voice was calmer than before and he sat down with a sigh in the recliner. "I told them, like you said. Don't know why they need to get mixed up in this business—they're just kids."

"Weren't you their age when you joined the mob on the hill? Children are capable of many things, good and evil," Wayne replied.

"Your parents were there too, youngin. Don't act like everyone else in this town is innocent," Murphy sniped back.

"They'll be caught up in it regardless of what they're told. We just wanted them to be prepared."

"I don't understand what good it will do them. Granny Bael's a force of nature. If she gets out, there won't be anyone to stop her." Murphy shivered and took his flask from his back pocket. His hands shook as he took a swig.

"We have a plan and a backup plan," Wayne said. "I hope it will be enough."

"Me too," Murphy replied. "Anything on the other front?"

"No. Abby's been digging, but she hasn't found anything. Some secrets are buried deeper than the dead."

"Shame. Maybe it's just as well Granny burns it all to the ground and brings an end to this madness."

"Have faith, my friend. We're setting things up here at the ranch. Talk again soon."

"All right," Murphy said and hung up the phone. He took another swig and closed his eyes.

He was back on the hill, surrounded by everyone in the town at the top of Grantham Point, the hill just south of town square. They all faced south as the cross Granny Balsom was tied to rose into the air.

"Hear me this night!" said the old man standing on the rock next to the cross so he could be seen by the milling crowd. Murphy recognized him as one of the town elders, Elwin Dawkins. He had a book in his hands and seemed to be holding it open. Beneath the cross, workers set up wood logs and bales of hay. "This witch has slaughtered her family in a wicked deal with the devil!"

The crowd hollered in support of Elwin's accusations. On the cross, Granny struggled but she'd been bound and gagged and could say nothing in her own defense. Even as the mob seemed to surge with anger, Murphy frowned. Elwin talked like he was a preacher, but hadn't he been instrumental in getting churches removed from the town? Enemies to free thought, he'd called them.

"You must all join in burning this witch to counter the evil spell she has cast upon this town!" Elwin said. "Gather a torch from the pile over there and throw it on the fuel under the witch Granny Balsom!"

After that, the crowd went crazy, grabbing torches and setting the cross and Granny Balsom alight. Murphy watched as Elwin's mouth moved, but he wasn't shouting to the crowd. He never knew exactly what Elwin said that night, but he had good reason to believe the old man was casting a spell himself and Granny Balsom was the catalyst for it. The Dawkins elders had total power over Tuggville from that night on and Murphy couldn't believe it was just a coincidence.

Even through the gag, Murphy could hear Granny screaming as the flames consumed her until she finally fell silent. The flames continued on late into the night, reducing everything including Granny's body to mere ash. In the morning, when most of the town had left and gone to sleep, Murphy remained behind and watched a work crew gather up all the ashes they could and transport it elsewhere. He didn't know where exactly until decades later when Granny returned at the old mill.

Murphy opened his eyes and took a deep swig of the burning liquid. He squinted hard as he swallowed it down. He could still hear her screams on the cross, just like he heard them every night in his dreams. Whatever curse she'd placed on the town that night had persisted. Everyone on the hill was adversely affected, whether by conscious or some dark spell cast upon them. No one in Tuggville was ever truly happy again.

5
SARCOPHAGUS

Officer Howard Tulley pulled the car up in front of the chain link fence. The gate for the fence still had a padlock on it, but the fence had seen better days. The bent, rusty metal was clearly breached in several spots and Howard sighed.

"Even the shit that ain't worth stealing gets snagged," he mumbled. He looked around to see if anyone was around. It was broad daylight; the perfect time to make his rounds at the District. He stepped over what remained of the fence at one of the breaches and walked into the complex of aging, broken down warehouse buildings. The cracked cement pavement was nearly crushed rock in many places. He stepped gingerly to avoid twisting an ankle on the broken surface.

He glanced in each of the buildings on his way through the complex, stopping and listening at each one. There was nothing but silence. Even the rodents and birds avoided this abandoned complex. Every once in a while, he'd shake one of the walls just to see what would come loose and fall. Most of the time, the steel and sheet metal structures still held together fairly well. None of them had intact roofs anymore and, while the fauna seemed to avoid the area, the flora was well entrenched here. Some of the buildings were little more than a façade surrounding a growing mini forest inside.

Behind the first two rows of buildings there was a large open area that had been used for piling up spoils from the quarry and moving trucks in and out. Some of the loading structures still survived, but none of them were usable. He doubted anyone could even climb on them without causing them to collapse to the ground.

At the far edge of the opening, there was a copse of trees and bushes encroaching on the cement. The foursome of teens hid in the shadows watching the police officer in the far distance approach a large dome of concrete nearly fifteen feet high and about as big around in the middle of the open area. They watched him walk slowly around the structure, carefully examining every inch.

"What's he looking for?" Dom whispered.

"He's your uncle, maybe you can ask him later?" Teek replied. Dom just shook his head.

Howard looked closely at a crack in the cement. He noticed several of them along the edge of the huge sarcophagus. He was careful not to touch any of the building. Broken chains lay around the buildings with rusted out signs warning of radioactivity. He reached one of the cracks that looked larger than the others.

"Well, that can't be good," he mumbled. "Stupid quakes.

Maybe we can patch it."

He studied the edges of the crack and noticed it seemed to be deteriorating. He stepped back and chewed on a thumbnail as he considered the crack. He shook his head and turned back toward the front of the complex.

As quickly as he could, he jumped through the opening in the fence and climbed into his car. He took off out of the area and drove back up the only road leading into the complex.

"Okay, he's gone," Teek said and stepped out onto the broken cement heading toward the huge sarcophagus.

As Dom took in a breath to protest, the girls jumped out onto the cement, quickly joining Teek in his advance. "Shit," Dom muttered and followed them.

As they got closer to the structure, the wind started whipping up, carrying autumn leaves with it. The kids gathered their thin coats around them against the sudden chill. The fractured and chunky ground leading to the huge dome was a bit treacherous. They went as fast as they could, but it was rough going. More than once, one of them stumbled and almost fell.

"This reminds me of football practice," Dom said.

"Some people are just lucky—at least you made the team," Teek said.

"Yeah, lucky. I'm supposed to bond with a bunch of dicks who bullied me growing up. Really lucky."

"So no scoop on what it's like to be one of the cool kids, then?" Teek asked as he leaped across a break in the concrete that look more like a drainage ditch. The bottom was filled with a muddy muck that smelled like decomposing skunks.

"I'll be sure to ask them right before they gang up on me and stuff me head first in a trash can… again," Dom said.

"Fucking Tuggville," Jemma said. She jumped across the ditch and almost lost her balance. Dom leaped over and caught her arm, helping her regain her balance.

"Thanks," she said quietly.

"My pleasure," Dom said softly and then quickly cleared his throat. "We gotta look out for each other, right?"

"Yeah," Jemma replied.

"Okay," Dom smiled at her and Jemma nearly lost her balance on the uneven ground again. That familiar yearning in her heart felt like it was going to burst out of her chest. She lingered on his eyes a moment too long for him to not notice. She quickly looked away and at the ground. "Tricky footing."

"Yeah," Dom whispered. "Tricky."

Teek got closest to the dome first and reached his hand out to touch the rough surface. The cement was pitted and there was exposed rebar, mostly just a small section, but it was starting to rust.

"Hey," Dom said as he stepped up next to Teek and pulled his hand away.

"What?" Teek asked.

"Look," Dom said as he pointed down to a broken length of rusted chain that held a metal sign. Dom pushed it over with his foot and revealed a radioactive warning sign.

"I think it's just a scare tactic," Teek said. "If it was really radioactive, they'd have better controls around it."

"Sure," Mary said. "Because Tuggville really has their shit together when it comes to public safety."

"Look, it might be fake, but let's just be careful okay?" Dom said.

"All right, man," Teek said. "I know you're just looking out for us. No harm, no foul."

They wandered around the edge until they reached the bigger crack in the cement. It looked like the cement around the edges was loose. Teek picked up one of the radioactive signs on the ground and started chipping away at the loose cement chunks. It didn't take long for him to expose the inner rebar and the chunks and dust began to fall away inside the structure.

"That's not exactly careful," Dom hissed. "We need to get out of here before my uncle comes back. Maybe he saw this hole and thought it needed patching or something."

"Why would he do that?" Teek asked as he continued to poke at the cement, but didn't seem to be making much progress.

"Radioactivity, public safety, he's still a cop, you know."

Teek pressed his nose against the opening and sniffed. "It doesn't smell radioactive," he said wrinkling his nose.

"Really, genius? What the fuck does radioactive smell like?" Dom hissed. He looked nervously at the fence where his uncle had come in.

"Well," Teek said almost in a trance. "That smells like… death."

"I'd guess radioactivity would smell like death. Let's get out of here before my uncle gets back."

Teek turned to argue when a small frail voice from within the cement sarcophagus called out. "Help me, Teek," the voice said and everyone froze. They slowly turned to look at the hole.

"How does it know my name?" Teek whispered.

"Dig... me... out," the voice said, stronger and more threatening.

"Nope," Teek said and started stumbling back toward the woods at a frantic pace. "I'm noping the fuck right outta here!"

The others followed Teek's lead and ran back to the forest, doing their best parkour stumble over the rough terrain. The rush of the adrenaline brought them through the concrete obstacle course without injury, but winded. They stopped to catch their breath.

"What... the hell... was that?" Jemma asked.

"That was sealed," Teek gasped. "How could anything be alive? How could it know my name?"

"Teeeeeeeeeeeeeeek!" a shrill voice screamed and echoed off the broken walls of the District buildings.

"Fuck! Fuck, fuck, fuck!" Teek cried out as he bolted into the forest. The others were right on his tail.

6

DENIAL

oward pulled up slowly to a stop in front of the quaint cottage at the end of the cul-de-sac. His eyes roamed over the circles of salt surrounding the building. He remembered the initial days of their construction years ago. Once while the workmen dug the trenches, he'd approached with the hope of getting a word with Abigail, but watched with despair as her wispy white dress disappeared into the house. He knew she'd retreated inside because he was attempting to reach her again.

He returned the next couple of days as construction continued, always staying at the end of the street. He caught glimpses of her, sometimes dressed in different colors, flitting around the work site talking to the workmen and pointing at the work they were doing. Howard kept his distance. It was the most he'd seen of his lost love in years.

One time, Howard brought a pair of binoculars with him and spotted her standing on the porch. When he brought the lenses up to his eyes, Abigail looked straight at him like she knew he was watching her. His breath caught in his throat at her beauty, her soft glowing face under wild curly blonde hair. It hadn't occurred to him to be suspicious of how she knew he was looking at her, he was just so glad to see her face again after so long even if it was from hundreds of feet away through magnification lenses. She shook her head at him and retreated again into the plainly decorated building. Even as a lump rose in his throat at her rejection, he kept the lenses focused on the house and took in all the odd decorations on the building. He noticed the outlines of dozens of different symbols and the first of what would be multiple affectations hanging around the building from dream catchers to crosses and other objects he didn't recognize. It didn't occur to him until years later that she was constructing a fortress of protection to keep out evil, or so he'd eventually surmised.

When the construction of the salt circles around the house were finished, so were Abby's appearances outside the cottage, at least for the next several days that he popped by. He noticed the symbols on the walls were more filled in and permanent as time went on and the objects hanging from the rafters increased in number every time he checked back in on her.

Howard's hands gripped the steering wheel tight enough that sweat began to bead on the back of his fingers. He relaxed his grip and dropped his hands into his lap. He glanced at the cottage door and grimaced.

It had been nearly twenty-five years since he'd felt her in his arms. He could still remember her scent, flowery and sweet. He cherished the feel of her soft curly hair against his cheek as she nuzzled herself into his chest. His pulse raced as that night came into focus for him again. She had been there to comfort him when his brother had died fighting Granny Bael. They defeated the old witch, but it had taken the life of one of their own in the process. It was like he'd lost an arm, seeing his brother die in an eruption of flame. If it hadn't been for Abigail, he might've drowned in a vortex of despair like his surviving brother had.

No other woman had received his affections since that night; Howard was pretty sure no other woman ever would. Abigail had his heart and soul forever even if they could never be together again.

His gaze fell back to the steering wheel. The round circle seemed to sway and shimmer in the car. He blinked his eyes quickly. His arms felt like lead and they fell to his sides. He squeezed his eyes shut and fought back the tears. He took a deep breath and let it out.

Her voice slid into his mind like a whisper. *My love, I'm sorry we can't be together ever again. I cannot help you with this task. Leave and never return. Find love and happiness far away from this place.*

Howard slumped forward in the seat and woke up with a start. Had he fallen asleep? The clock on the dash showed thirty minutes had passed. He shook his head to clear the cobwebs and opened the car door.

He stepped out of the car and looked again at the cottage. The light on the porch illuminated the area with a pure white light. He blinked as his mind traveled back to their high school days when Abigail would leave the slightly yellow porch light on if her parents were asleep or weren't home. It was their understood signal that he could come and get her to leave on whatever adventures they might find with their friends or with just the two of them.

He stepped around the car and walked up the front path. He rapped his knuckles on the front door and stepped back.

"Abby!" he shouted. "I don't know what I've done and I'm sorry. Besides our troubles, I think Granny Bael might be coming back and I need your help."

The porch light went off and Howard's heart sank. He waited for a few seconds, but there was no reply from within.

Inside the cottage, Abigail watched Howard from behind the cover of a curtained window in a darkened room. Tears streamed down her face, but she didn't move from her spot. Every memory Howard had of their love, their connection, their bond beyond time and space, she felt it too within every fiber of her being. But the path forward couldn't be together. She'd foreseen it and it tore her insides apart to be away from him.

"Please!" Howard cried. "I miss you!"

Howard waited for several more minutes before he finally turned, head hung down as he slowly returned to his patrol car.

Abigail moved within the room to change her vantage point so she could watch him as he climbed into his car and departed.

"The war is upon us, sweet knight," she whispered. "Stay strong, be fierce and be brave."

After Howard disappeared from her sight, she stood there for what seemed to her forever, staring at the empty cul-de-sac and feeling it reflected her soul in its emptiness and darkness.

Finally, she turned from the window and returned to her inner sanctuary. The room was dark except for the flicker of a dozen candles around the room. She navigated the room expertly, memorized in the thousands of times she'd traversed it. She walked to the center of the room and sat down in a cross-legged pose and centered herself. She closed her eyes and controlled her breathing. She concentrated on her memories, deftly navigating around the pain and darkness that came just two days after they'd defeated, no, trapped Granny Bael. She traveled back to the only happy times she'd known in life. Howard figured in nearly all of them. She rejoiced in his touch, his laugh, and his love. She buried her psyche in the memories of those days in high school when they first professed their love and the joyous months afterwards.

She had to revisit the memories every once in a while to keep her mind aloft and out of the dark places she'd been to both against her will and voluntarily. Her time with the true monster of Tuggville had forced her to reconsider the role of Granny Bael in the overall scheme of the dark happenings of the town. She felt a strange affinity for the killer of her lover's brother. Like Granny Bael, Abigail was also victim and villain.

7
NO SANCTUARY

They ran and ran until their lungs burned, desperate to escape the unnamed horror that had called out Teek's name from the darkness. They slowed down to catch their breath, but kept moving until their legs brought them to the abandoned farm and derelict barn they loosely called a refuge from the outside world.

Teek went in first, followed by the girls. Dom squeezed himself through the opening and then pushed the door closed, brushing off the fallen dust and splinters as he always did. Teek collapsed on one of the hay bales in the little shelter and just lay there catching his breath with his eyes closed tight. Mary and Jemma sat down on another set of bales and just sat looking at the ground.

Dom walked into the little shelter and sat down with a huff.

"What the fuck was that?" Dom asked. Of all of them, he was the least out of breath. Football conditioning had prepared him for running and stressful situations, although the training regime was likely never designed for this.

"That was Granny Bael," Teek whispered. Jemma jumped up, shocking Dom and Mary. Teek still lay on his stomach.

"The fuck it is, Teek!" Jemma screamed. "You think this little prank is funny? You get Old Man Murphy to tell us some fucked up tale about our families killing somebody and then setup this stupid prank to scare us? You think this is fucking funny, Teek?"

Teek turned around and sat up, but didn't meet Jemma's eyes. "It's not a prank," Teek said.

"The hell it isn't, Teek!" Jemma hollered and looked at Mary and Dom. "What, are you two in on it too? You think my shitty life isn't fucked up enough without having to worry about disembodied voices fucking with me?"

"It's not a prank!" Teek shouted and stood up. "You're all my family! I wouldn't do that to you! You're all I have!"

Jemma looked at Teek and the anger faded almost instantly. As sorrow and fear collided in her mind, tears welled in her eyes and started running down her cheeks. Teek rushed over to Jemma and hugged her. Mary and Dom got up too and they all hugged each other.

"I'm sorry, Teek," Jemma whispered. "I'm just scared."

"Me too," Teek whispered.

"Well, I think we're all a little fucking scared," Mary quipped and they all laughed together as the tears flowed.

The ground suddenly shook for a moment and a board from the barn roof fell onto the little shelter. They all jumped when it hit the roof of the shelter. They looked around and a cascade of dust floated down into the air around them.

"Might not be safe here anymore," Dom said. "You guys stay here and I'll go open the door. When I holler, run for it."

They all nodded in agreement. Dom ran to the big door and tried to push it open. Something had shifted in the minor tremor and he couldn't get it open more than a foot. He looked around the barn floor and found a thick timber that didn't appear too rotted. He picked it up, jammed it into the opening and pried the door open until it was big enough for him to wedge his arm and shoulder in the gap. He set his feet and pushed with everything he had. The door slid open.

Dom looked up at the roof of the barn for a moment and then waved his friends to the door.

"Let's go!" he rasped.

They ran to the opening and everyone got out of the barn in one piece. As they stepped away from it, they heard a large crack and ran. The old barn they used for a meeting place for the last six years crumbled into debris in an instant.

When they were a safe distance away, they stopped and turned around.

"Well, shit," Mary said.

"This sucks," Teek added.

"Hey," Dom said as he grabbed them both in a hug. "At least we have each other. That was just a building."

Jemma smiled and joined in the hugfest. When they all broke it off and turned to leave, she looked at the building once more.

"Then why does it feel like everything's coming apart?" she whispered.

8

DUTY

Diedre struggled fitfully as nightmares swarmed through her mind and pulled her down into the darkness. She couldn't move. A heavy weight on top of her kept her prone. She felt a piercing stab and couldn't breathe. Progressively urgent grunting sounds brought tears to her eyes. The smell of candles and something darker, smokier filled her nostrils. She gasped for air; nothing but pain and despair filled her lungs.

She sat up, fully awake. The memories flooded back in. She held her head and screamed.

Downstairs, Jemma had just returned from the District. She was shaken by the experience and jumped when she heard her mom scream.

"Mom?" Jemma shouted as she rushed to the stairs. Her little four year old brother, David, and six year old sister, Martha, poked their heads out of their rooms. Diedre came storming out of her room in pajamas and slippers. She ran down the stairs, passing Jemma without a word. She went into the kitchen. Jemma followed her.

"Mom, what's wrong?"

"He's in my head, Jemma. I can feel him on me, in me. I can't make him go away!" Diedre shouted and pulled down a bottle of vodka from the cabinet. It was nearly empty. She opened the bottle and drank the last of it straight. "There's no more vodka! I don't want to feel him anymore!"

"Who, Mom? Who is it?" Jemma shouted.

Diedre looked at her daughter with nearly sober eyes and tears streamed down her face. "I don't know!"

Diedre dropped the bottle on the counter and walked to the front door. She opened the closet, grabbed her jacket and ran out of the house. Jemma walked to the door and watched her mom climb into her car and peel out, speeding out of their cul-de-sac. Neighbors appeared on their porches and watched the departing vehicle. They looked back at Jemma standing helplessly in the door way. They all shook their heads sadly and went back inside. It was just another Sunday to them.

Jemma closed the door. She looked at the stairs and saw her dark haired siblings looking at her with concern. They both looked like they were on the verge of tears. "Hey, have you guys eaten anything yet?" Jemma asked gently. "Come with me and we'll make you something, okay?" The little ones nodded and followed Jemma into the kitchen without a word.

When Jemma got into the kitchen, she looked at the empty vodka bottle on the counter and paused. She grabbed the bottle and tossed it into the trash can. She turned to her siblings and smiled.

"You want some pancakes?"

Howard pulled up in the nearly empty parking lot of the strip mall. Of the five shops, two were vacant with leasing signs and two were salons bordering a small office with a bold red and black sign that said Phalanx Insurance Agency. He parked his car across from the insurance agency and held onto the steering wheel for a few moments, steadying his breathing.

"You can do this," Howard repeated in a self affirming chant. After a few repetitions, he got out of the car and walked across to the agency. He pulled open the door and a professional ginger-haired middle-aged woman looked up smiling. The smile faded quickly when she saw who it was. A young black woman looked up from her desk; she was maybe half the ginger haired woman's age. The younger woman got up and approached Howard with a big smile.

"How can Phalanx Insurance Agency help you today?"

"Hi, I'm actually here to see—" Howard began to say.

"Bridget?" the older woman said abruptly, but professionally. "Could you run to the coffee shop and bring back two lattes and get something for yourself? Officer Tulley is not here on insurance business, are you Officer?"

"Uh, no," Howard mumbled.

"Okay," Bridget said brightly. She grabbed her phone and walked out the door.

"Shanna, I—" Howard said. Shanna cut him off with a glare as she walked by him and locked the door. She flipped the sign in the window to 'Closed.'

"Won't you come with me to the conference room?" she said sweetly as she walked by him.

"Uh, sure," Howard said as he followed her.

At the back of the small office were two doors, one to each side. The frosted glass on the one office with the closed door read: "Rick Roman, President, Phalanx Insurance Agency." Shanna walked to the other side with the open door and the clear windows. Inside was a small conference table that sat four people comfortably.

"Uh, shouldn't Rick be joining us?" Howard said hesitating.

"All in good time, Officer Tulley," Shanna said sporting a clean, professional grin meant to put prospective customers at ease. It had the opposite effect on Howard and he felt his insides begin to turn. He walked into the conference room and sat down in a chair with his back to the window as Shanna directed. She shut the door, walked to the opposite side of the conference table and sat down. She pulled out a set of insurance brochures and spread them across the table.

"I'm not here to buy insurance," Howard said.

"Oh, I know. They're for Rick's benefit so he doesn't get suspicious about why I'm in here alone with a police officer," Shanna said. She smiled that professional smile again, all sales, no emotion.

"We could just tell him," Howard said.

"No!" Shanna hissed. "He doesn't need this kind of pressure. It's hard enough making it as a business in this town! His blood pressure is through the roof. Last thing he needs is to go chasing ghosts."

Howard leaned forward and lifted up a life insurance brochure. "We made a life pact that day," Howard said. "We'd never let Edward's sacrifice be forgotten, never let it be in vain. We all need to honor that contract."

Howard leaned across the small table and set the brochure in front of Shanna. "You know how to honor contracts, right?"

Shanna looked up with venom in her eyes. "I notice you're here alone, Howard," Shanna said. Howard watched the vein in her temple pulse madly. "Didn't Abigail want to play or have you not gone to see her yet?"

"I'm going to see her, but…"

"But that night drove her insane," Shanna finished. "So, you value her life over Rick's."

"It's not like that," Howard protested.

"Isn't it?" Shanna sat back in the chair and folded her arms. "Wouldn't return our phone calls, won't answer the door, and look at her house now—a ramshackle cacophony of salt circles and totems. She's the most paranoid person in town and that's saying something for Tuggville."

Howard tapped his fingers on the table and looked down. He took a deep breath. For just the briefest moment, his feelings for Abigail jumped to his surface thoughts. He cherished those memories of holding hands during school assemblies, kicking back by the river and, of course, getting ice cream at the grocery store to the utter disgust of that racist thug Cary Deering. He absolutely loved Abigail flaunting their budding relationship in front of Cary, leaving him sputtering racist nonsense and getting the cold shoulder from most of the others in school. He was certain they'd be together forever until she disappeared that day after graduation and came back changed. He'd never forget the haunted look in her eyes when she shrunk away from his touch and told him they couldn't see each other anymore.

"I think she knows things are happening in the District. She sent me something last year—a note that said 'The veil is falling, she's growing stronger.' I've been checking the sarcophagus every day since then and it's starting to crumble."

"Then you should contact Dawkins and get him to fix it," Shanna said. "Problem solved. Then I don't have to play Abby's part pouring salt and doing some stupid incantations."

"She sent you something too?" Howard asked.

"Last year, but I'm not doing it. We're done with that," Shanna said. "Put another layer of cement on the thing and be done with it."

"Maybe you should call Dawkins, he was always sweet on you," Rick said from the doorway, making them both jump.

"Rick! Uh, Officer Tulley was just leaving. He's going to come back and talk about bundling his insurance with us next week," Shanna said standing up.

Rick ran a hand through his thinning blonde hair and smiled. "We'll be there if we're needed, Howard," Rick said.

"Rick, please," Shanna begged.

"We're all living on borrowed time, Shanna," Rick said. He walked around the table and grabbed her shoulders gently. "We put the genie in the bottle, trapped it, but we didn't destroy it. We can't let it get back out."

Shanna slumped into Rick's arms. "Please, Rick, no. We didn't create the genie. It isn't our responsibility," Shanna whispered.

"Evil begets evil," Howard said as he stood up.

"What?" Rick asked. "Granny Bael was already evil when they burned her at the stake."

"I don't know." Howard shrugged. "It was the last thing Abby said before she… slammed the door in my face and stopped talking to all of us."

"Great. Crazy, cryptic Abby leaves us to pick up the pieces," Shanna said.

"Look, I'm going to pick up a couple bags of cement and patch up those holes. She's still trapped. We should be fine," Howard said.

"You really think that's going to hold up against these fucking quakes?" Rick asked. "Fracking to save the town. Tuggville should've just died a natural death."

"There was a fairly significant crack, but it hadn't gone all the way through. As long as nothing disturbs what's inside, it shouldn't matter. I'll shore it up tomorrow. I just wanted you two to be in on the loop."

"I think Dawkins should contribute some of his profits to making the entire District a cement slab," Rick replied. "Pretty sure he's the one behind the fracking, selling this town out to the highest bidder. All that land is owned by some shadow corporation I haven't been able to get past."

There was a knock at the front door. Shanna put her head up and resumed the bearing of a professional.

"I think that's our coffee and your cue to leave, Officer

Tulley. Give Abigail our best, won't you?" Shanna said the last with a venomous iciness that made Howard shudder. She walked out of the conference room and walked to the front door.

"Rick, I didn't mean to make things awkward," Howard said as he pushed the chair in.

"A bat shit crazy recluse is supposed to be our ally against an ancient evil," Rick said as he stepped out of the room. "It was awkward before you walked in."

9
HERALDS

When Mary got home, she found her mother snoozing in the chair.

"Hi Mary," Gwen said from behind her. Mary shrieked and quickly covered her mouth.

"Sorry," Mary whispered as she turned around. Gwen, the other home care nurse, was on her hands and knees next to the china cabinet cleaning up with a broom and dustpan. Mary noticed one of the large serving dishes was missing.

"That little quake knocked a few items off," Gwen said. "Your mother wasn't hurt, but I'm afraid you've lost a few dishes here." Gwen pointed up at the lower shelf and Mary noticed two tea cups missing as well.

"It's okay, Gwen," Mary replied. She looked over at her mother. "I don't think we're going to be having any more dinner parties."

Gwen stood up with a groan. Mary rushed over to take the dustpan and broom from her and help her up from the floor.

"Thank you, Mary," Gwen said and patted Mary on the shoulder. "Let's go in the kitchen and dump that. I have a paper sack for all the broken pieces."

They walked into the kitchen and Gwen took the dustpan and dumped the pieces into the sack where they clinked with the other pieces inside. She handed the dustpan back to Mary, who put the tools away in the utility closet just off the kitchen. Gwen sat down at the dining room table and waved for Mary to come over.

"You know, Mary," Gwen said. "You need to prepare yourself. Your mother's not going to be here for much longer."

Mary sat down and stared at the table. Gwen sat patiently and smiled. "That's not what's bugging me. I mean, that sucks, but I think I've come to accept that," Mary said.

"Then what is it, child? You're not usually this upset when I see you."

"The dreams are getting worse," Mary said.

Gwen stiffened a bit and then forced herself to relax. "You know I don't believe in that stuff," Gwen replied. "Maybe you should talk to your aunt."

"Years ago, when we still got together occasionally, she said it runs in the family," Mary replied.

"I take it back. You shouldn't talk to your aunt. Crazy doesn't 'run in the family.' You just need to rest." Gwen patted Mary's hand and stood up. "I need to go and do some grocery shopping before I get home. I'm out of milk."

"I need to know what it means," Mary said.

"She's filling your head with nonsense," Gwen hissed.

"This psychic mumbo jumbo is just a scam. I once had a psychic tell me I would marry a rich man and look at me now, no husband and talking to crazy people all day."

Mary giggled. Gwen huffed and then giggled too. She hugged Mary and went to get her coat and purse. Mary sat there for a while looking at the table and zoning out the best she could. When Gwen returned, coat on and purse in hand, she set her hand on Mary's shoulder.

"When your mother passes, I will be leaving Tuggville. It's been three years and I don't have a good feeling here. You should think about leaving too."

Mary stood up and walked Gwen to the front door. "It's been on my mind. I don't know why we've stayed so long," Mary said and hugged Gwen again.

"I'll see you day after tomorrow," Gwen said as she stepped out the door. Mary let the screen door swing almost shut before catching it with her toe and letting it close quietly. She watched Gwen walk to her bicycle resting against the garage door. Gwen got on the bicycle and rode away.

Suddenly, Mary reached out to the screen door, her face suddenly white as she watched Gwen go up in flames in front of her eyes for a moment and then return to normal.

"Gwen," she whispered and then let her hand fall. "I won't be seeing you again." She clenched her jaw and shut the front door. "Dammit, Aunt Abby! What's happening to me?" Mary whispered.

In the darkness of the room, she heard her mother stir. Mary went to her side and kneeled down next to her. "Mom?" Mary asked. "Are you comfortable? Do you need anything?"

Her mother opened her eyes a little and raised her hand up to Mary's cheek. "I'm okay," her mother said as she dropped her hand back down to her lap. "I'll just rest here."

Mary patted her mom's hand. Her mom turned away from her and shut her eyes. Mary was a few steps away when she heard her mom sigh and she turned back around.

"It's too bad about Gwen," her mother said sleepily. "I really liked her."

She walked quickly back to her mother, but she had fallen completely asleep again. Mary sighed and walked back into the kitchen. She grabbed a water bottle from the fridge and drank half of it down. She closed her eyes and tears formed.

"Shit," she whispered. She put the water back and went to her bedroom.

Teek opened the back door to the second house on the Macpherson property. He moved as quietly as he could, but Jasper Macpherson snuck up behind him and grabbed him by the nape of the neck.

"Nice of you to join us for dinner, boy!" Jasper hollered and Teek wrinkled his nose. Jasper had been drinking and the alcoholic stench made Teek's eyes water. The older man dressed in overalls, an old red flannel shirt and brand new cowboy boots shoved his foster son forward. Teek stumbled down the hallway and into the so-called dining room.

The dining room in the second house was comprised of three outdoor picnic tables strung together in a row. Thirteen other kids of varying ages from three to seventeen years old were gathered at the table. The younger ones sniffled like they'd been crying for a while and were exhausted from it. The older kids looked sullen and pale. It was easy to tell some of them were a little malnourished, even in the dim light from the two, one-bulb ceiling lamps on the walls at either end of the long table.

Teek wasn't used to seeing all of them gathered together at the table for dinner. They usually ate in shifts, depending on what food was available. The room stank of garlic and puke. The surface of the table and the surrounding floor was spattered with liquids that all shared the same various shade of yellow green.

Jasper grabbed Teek's arm hard and shoved him toward the table.

"Have a seat, boy," he growled. Then the lanky, bearded man turned toward the kitchen as Teek climbed onto one of the benches. He looked around the table and noticed some of the older kids were sporting fat lips and bloody noses.

'Oh shit, it's gonna be one of those kind of nights,' Teek thought.

"Martha, we got another lovely young man gracing us with his presence for dinner!" Jasper hollered toward the kitchen.

Martha came out dressed in a white apron spattered with yellow liquid. She had the sleeves of her blue floral blouse rolled up. Teek noticed her designer jeans were spotless, but her shiny black boots were spattered with a little bit of the same fluid that was on the apron. She set a bowl down in front of Teek along with a spoon.

"Everybody else has already partaken, boy," Jasper said as

he got down next to Teek's face. "Pretty rude to stand us all up for dinner, don't you think?"

Jasper flicked Teek's ear and Teek squeaked in pain.

"Now eat up! We got us a family gathering to start," Jasper said.

Teek looked around the table, but none of the kids would meet his gaze. They all looked down or away from Teek.

"I'm not really hungry," Teek replied. Jasper smacked him upside the back of the head.

"We feeding you too much, boy?"

"No sir," Teek replied.

"Then you better eat or I'm going to start beating little Sally here until she can't walk," Jasper yelled.

"Alright!" Teek shouted. "I'll eat!" Teek picked up the spoon. None of the kids would look his direction except for Barbara, the oldest, who glanced sideways at him with tears in her eyes.

Teek took a sip of the soup. It was so heavy with garlic he might as well be gnawing on a garlic clove. There were little bits of some kind of meat floating in the liquid that he thought might be chicken, but with the heavy garlic flavor he couldn't really tell.

"Now, it seems someone alerted authorities that Danny was missing," Jasper announced to the room. One of the middle aged kids looked at Teek, then turned his head and threw up on the floor behind him. Teek thought his name was Jesse, but they never spoke much.

"I don't take kindly to outsiders knowing our business," Jasper said. "I wanted to call this family meeting to remind all of you to keep your little fucking mouths shut about what goes on inside these walls. Do I make myself clear?"

Everyone mumbled a 'yes' and Teek started to agree, but felt something funny in his stomach. He looked down at the bowl and realized he'd eaten about half of the soup. He set the spoon down.

"This soup may or may not include pieces of your dear missing brother, Danny," Jasper said. The five oldest kids turned their heads from the table and vomited on the floor. The poor little middle aged kid, Jesse, did again as well. Teek pushed the bowl away and felt a little green.

No, it was more than that. It felt like someone had stabbed him in the stomach and was slowly turning the knife.

"May or may not," Martha said as she leaned against the doorway leading to the kitchen. She laughed and so did Jasper.

Teek's stomach couldn't take what was happening and he vomited right onto the top of the table. But, it wasn't a quick one and done. He retched again and again as his gut twisted in knots. He couldn't even turn from the table; he just tried to hold onto something so he didn't fall onto the floor. Tears came to his eyes and he could barely acknowledge the laughter coming from the Macphersons as he emptied the contents of his stomach and then began dry heaving.

After fifteen minutes, Teek laid his head on the table. He just gasped and burped, hoping the next burp wasn't vomit. His head was smeared with the thick viscous liquid contents of his stomach.

"Now that we've all joined in this little bonding session, I would remind you little pukes," Jasper said, but couldn't continue as he and Martha fell into a laughing fit at his impromptu joke.

Little Sally fell to the floor, passed out. The induced vomit and abuse had been too much for her. Jasper growled at her. "Any of you that says a goddamn thing about what happens in this house will become the next meal! Whatever you don't eat, I'll just feed to the pigs down the road. Farmer Kyle loves free food for his little oinkers."

Jasper wrinkled his nose and turned toward the front door. "Now clean yourselves up. You fucking stink," he said and laughed as he walked out the door. Martha walked out with him, stopping briefly to look at Sally out cold on the floor. She gave a little humph and left the building. She didn't try to help the toddler or even appear concerned about her well-being.

After a few minutes, some of the kids got up. The older ones helped the younger ones to the sink in the kitchen, where the only running water was in the house. They were able to rouse Sally with some cool water and gentle talking. She woke and cried, but quickly stopped. She was clearly frightened any outburst could result in more abuse, even though the abusers had left.

Everyone stripped down to their underwear and rinsed off with buckets of cold water. They soaped down with the underwear on and just rinsed off like it was a bathing suit. It was something they did automatically like they'd done it a hundred times before because they had.

"I'm sorry, Teek," Barbara said as she touched Teek's head

gently. "He threatened us if we said anything and—"

"It's okay," Teek slurred as he held up a hand. "Not your fault."

He pushed himself up and just held himself there for a moment as Barbara went to go clean up with the others. Fluid dripped off his face and he blinked his eyes hard to try to clear the tears.

"Didn't think the day could get worse," Teek whispered as he leaned on the table and rested his head in his hands. "That was fucking stupid."

Dom walked in and heard the television in the living room playing the news. He frowned. His good for nothing step father never watched the news. He walked through the dining room and entered the living room.

Dom's mom sat on the couch with an ice pack pressed onto her face. She still wore her nurse's uniform from the hospital, but red stains of blood ran down the left hand side. Dom clenched his fists but kept his composure.

"Mom, you all right?" Dom asked gently.

His mom jumped a little at his voice, but then turned to look at him with the eye that wasn't covered by the ice pack. He walked into the living room and saw Marv passed out on the floor. He noticed the blood on Marv's right hand. He stepped gingerly over the snoring thug.

"I'm fine," his mom said. "Just fell coming in the house."

"Mom, you need to leave him," Dom said softly as he sat on the couch next to her.

His mom grinned a little and winced. "It's not his fault,"

she said. "I told him the television wouldn't be in until next week. I should've just gotten the damn display in the window. I should've insisted. It's all my fault."

"Mom," Dom protested, but she held up her hand.

"Not another word about it," she stated. "You should just go to your room and have a good night's rest. I have to leave for work in an hour and I'm going to have to change."

She got up from the couch and steadied herself on the arm of the couch for a moment.

"Can't let the staff see this mess, then they'll really know how clumsy I am. Might get fired!" she said and laughed as she walked out of the room. Dom got up and followed her.

"Mom, we can both just get our stuff, climb in the car and leave. Get out of Tuggville forever," Dom said even as a lump formed in his throat when he thought about leaving Jemma behind. Maybe he could convince her to go too.

"We can't leave Tuggville!" his mother screamed at him. The effort made her dizzy and she leaned on the wall for support. "Do you know why your father drinks?"

"Marv isn't my father," Dom said.

"I'm not talking about Marv, honey," she said. "Your father drinks to block out the pain."

"I know. He's messed up about Uncle Edward."

"No, that's why he left, but the drinking is so he can ignore the siren call drawing him back," his mother walked into her bedroom and sat on the bed. "We all feel it when we try to leave, baby. It's a yearning that starts in your head, tugs at your soul and burns like fire if you ignore it. Your father puts out the fire with whiskey so he can stay away."

"That's ridiculous," Dom said.

His mother looked down at the floor. "I went with him when he first left," she said. "I felt it too. I tried to drink it away like he did, but I couldn't. It just didn't work for me. I had to come back. I had to leave him there."

"What?" Dom asked. "I don't remember leaving Tuggville."

"You were a year old," she said as she smiled grimly. "I left you with Grandma Tulley. Taking care of you made her so happy. She almost forgot about Edward when she had you bouncing on her lap. Or maybe, she just pretended you were Edward. She pretended she hadn't lost him."

She lowered the ice pack and set it on the bed. Her left eye was swollen shut, she had a cut under her eye and her lip was swollen. Her lip was broken open and there was a trail of dried blood leading down to her chin.

"We're all cursed by Tuggville, Dom. A living hell we can never escape. We just try to make the best of it that we can," she said. She stood up and looked at him with a shrug. "I'm not perfect. Your father isn't perfect. Marv sure as hell isn't perfect!"

"I'll say," Dom added. They both chuckled for a moment. The laughs were accompanied by tears.

"We just have to make do with the hand we've been dealt, Dom." She waved at him to leave. "Now get out of here so I can get changed."

Dom left the room and his mother closed the door. He stood at the door for several minutes just breathing and trying to control the burning hate rising up inside of him. He listened to his mother puttering around her bedroom, squeaking in pain every once in a while as she likely touched her damaged face while she changed clothes.

Dom walked out into the living room. He looked down at the man who had just beaten his mother and slumbered fitfully, so drunk he couldn't even stand. He looked back at his mother's room and felt his jaw tighten.

He walked around Marv until he stared at the bloody hand Marv had beaten his mother with. He stepped on the hand and hopped up and down once on it, feeling and hearing the bones crack. Marv stirred and moaned but was so drunk even having his hand broken didn't wake him.

"Hope you can work the remote with your other hand, asshole," Dom said and walked out of the room.

Jemma sat on the recliner watching her mother passed out on the couch. The half empty bottle of vodka sat on the coffee table in front of the couch, lid nowhere to be found. Diedre's hair was a tangled mess flopped over her sweaty brow. Her nostrils flared as she breathed in and out heavily.

"This is going to kill you, Mom," Jemma said quietly. "What horrible thing happened to you to make you do this?"

Diedre had aged far beyond her thirty-five years. She'd gained wrinkles a woman her age shouldn't have and her jet black hair started to gray at the edges. She'd lost a bunch weight in the last year—so much so that Jemma was surprised she could handle all the alcohol she consumed.

"I wish I could talk to you, Mom," Jemma said, tears welling up in her eyes. "There's some strange stuff going down. There are earthquakes, voices from the past, and some old dude spouting history that doesn't seem right. And you're blissfully drunk through all of it. Now that I say it out loud, you seem to be the most logical person in Tuggville."

She got up and walked over to Diedre, pushing the hair that had fallen onto her face back over her head. "I wish I could help make that pain go away, whatever it is."

Toys crashed together with screams of delight from upstairs where her little brother and sister played, oblivious to the slow-motion suicide their mother was engaged in. Outside, Jemma's father drove up into the driveway. The quick grind and click of him setting the emergency brake made her turn her head toward the front door. She could already imagine the shouting. Whether her mother would even respond was beyond her. Diedre had really tied one on this time.

"I'm going to be with the little ones," Jemma said as she gently touched her mom's cheek. "I can't imagine Dad will be happy when he sees you like this again." She got up to go and Diedre's hand grabbed her arm. Jemma squeaked.

"I'm sorry," her mother slurred. "It's in you. I couldn't stop him."

"What?" Jemma asked. But her mother's grasp loosened and her hand fell to the ground. "Mom? What are you talking about?" The car door slammed shut outside. Jemma looked at the front door and then back at her mom. "Shit!" Jemma hissed and rushed out of the living room.

10
SCHOOLED

Teek stood outside the school entrance just taking in the absurdity of it all. Rather than a center of learning, the building had taken on the center of abuse for him. The neglect and abuse he experienced at home combined with the horrors he faced here were nearly too much to bear on a daily basis. But, the threat of spending time locked up in the basement for missing even a single minute of the school day was enough to propel him forward. The basement was the last place he'd seen Danny go; the place where their psycho foster parents had stuck him for getting a D on a quiz. Two days passed and the basement was miraculously open. Danny was nowhere to be found. He shuddered to think they may have actually served him up as dinner. It made his stomach do a loop.

He pointlessly looked in the direction of his foster home. He couldn't see it from here, but he could feel the ominous presence around him everywhere. Danny was the only kid he knew to go missing, but rumors from the older kids before him reminded him he wasn't the first. The Macphersons had been foster parents for over twenty years and by the rumor mill, if Danny stayed missing, he'd be the fourth kid to do so.

How could there not be investigations? How could they keep on being foster parents when kids went missing under their care? He remembered one night talking to Jake before he left the home for good when he turned eighteen. The Macphersons had disappeared one of his foster siblings before Teek had come under their care. The police had come for a visit. They talked to the parents for five minutes and then Jake never saw them come to the house again. But all the kids had gone without food for the next two days as punishment for someone talking about the family outside their home. Even the babies had gone hungry as a lesson to the older ones that anyone could be disappeared at any minute and they didn't care how old the child was.

He was certain starving foster kids was likely a crime, but if they could get away with murder or selling kids off to who knew where with no repercussions, he sure wasn't going to bother reporting any crimes to anyone. They'd never pay for their crimes. He sighed and looked back at his next best option in life—getting bullied at high school.

Great options, he thought.

Teek trudged into the school hefting his backpack that carried books and paper but no food for lunch. He was lucky he qualified for free school lunches and could get those relatively easily. The school also provided breakfast, but he couldn't get that unscathed. The school bullies targeted him for many reasons and the nearly unsupervised breakfast line was a prime opportunity for them to vent their wrath. Hot eggs dropped down the back of your shirt or hot oatmeal splattered in your face was deterrent enough to seek breakfast elsewhere if at all.

"Hey Teek," one of the cheerleaders said as she passed. It was Erica, the captain of the squad and sometime girlfriend of several football players. "Who's your daddy?"

The blonde leader of the pep squad laughed along with the two other cheerleaders who walked with her past Teek into the entrance of the school. It was an old joke. He'd been teased since middle school ever since they found out no one knew who his father was. He sighed again. At least they hadn't badmouthed his mother in a long time. Maybe even these rat turds had some respect for the dead.

As he reached up for his locker, two passing kids bumped into him forcefully, knocking him against the lockers. A third villain tripped him and pushed him over, his face scraping against the locker and opening a small gash in his cheekbone. As Teek grabbed at his face and screamed, the three villains laughed and shouted, "Watch your step, loser!" before they disappeared down the hallway.

Teek's head was spinning when he felt a gentle grasp on his shoulder. "Teek, are you okay?" Teek recognized the voice as Mary's. The shame he felt was mixed with anger at the bullies.

He turned his face toward Mary and she gasped when she saw the blood. She grabbed his bag and pulled Teek up to his feet. "Come on, you're going to the nurse," Mary said. Teek thought about resisting, but there was blood streaming down his face and he figured there really wasn't much point. He'd be sent there one way or the other. Besides, Mary was a force of nature when she wanted to get her way.

"Thanks," he mumbled and shuffled along with Mary. She was perhaps the only upside to getting his face split open by the bully patrol.

Jemma sat down with a sigh in Physics as the rest of the class shuffled in. She opened up her book when a hand plopped down on it, class ring shining in the light. She lifted her head up and looked at the blonde short cropped hair of Eric Deering as he plopped himself down backwards on the chair of the desk in front of her. He smiled his smarmiest grin.

"Hey rich bitch, you're looking good today, how about getting together under the bleachers later so I can show you what a real man can do to you?"

"I'm not rich, Eric. You need someone with money to get it up? I'm not your girl."

"Look you little—" Eric started but a large dark-skinned hand grabbed his letterman jacket and pulled him up off the chair.

"She's not your girl, Eric. Didn't you hear?" Dom said.

"Well, Jemma, I didn't know you loved nig—" Eric started again.

"Do we have a problem, Mister Deering and Mister Tulley?" The physics teacher, Mister Graves asked as he turned around and saw the commotion. Dom let go of Eric's jacket.

"No problem, Eric just got lost going to his desk," Dom said.

"Good. It's too early in the morning to be handing out detentions. I haven't had my coffee yet," Mister Graves replied. He turned back to the chalkboard and continued writing notes for the class.

"I deal with you later, DUMBinique," Eric sneered and walked over to his own desk.

"Thank you, Dom," Jemma said quietly. "But what about after school?"

"He'll be too busy. Everyone knows he has weed in his locker. It's about time someone narced on him. Anonymously, of course."

"Damn," Jemma said with a grin.

"Yeah, about time someone pushed back," Dom said. He walked to the side of the room opposite Eric and took his own seat. He fished out his physics book from his backpack and set it on the table. The book was well worn and Dom smiled. He'd been through it a dozen times and memorized nearly every page. He had big plans to escape the football drudgery and get a science scholarship, maybe even to Alabama. He was on his way to valedictorian again this year, despite the objections from his stepfather.

He briefly considered if going into psychology might help him get the worthless leech that was Marv to leave under his own power. It shouldn't be too difficult to get a one track mind like Marv's to follow some rabbit down a hole to football glory. But, getting Marv to give up his cushy life might be too much of an obstacle. He'd just have to bide his time until the man's alcoholism shredded his liver. It was just two or three cases of beer a day, but he also drowned his pea brain in whiskey when he went out on the weekends with his buddies. Marv's days were definitely limited.

Nurse Rodriguez pressed the bloody gauze against the wound on Teek's face as he winced.

"You might need stitches," she said.

"Okay, go for it," Teek said.

"I can't do stitches at school. You'll have to go to the emergency room," she replied.

"I can't do that. My foster parents will shit a brick," Teek said.

"Dammit, you're one of the Macpherson kids? I'm sorry," She reached over into her drawer. "Okay, what I'm going to do for you is put these bandages on your face. They're very sticky, but should hold the wound closed so it can heal. You're lucky the cut isn't that deep."

She applied the bandages and they took up a bit of space on Teek's face. "Have you had a tetanus shot?" she asked.

"Two years ago, car accident. Foster parents' fault, so they couldn't get away with no one going to the hospital."

Nurse Rodriguez folded her arms and nodded. "Strangely fortunate, but one less thing to worry about, I guess. You come back tomorrow and I'll check that for you, and change the bandages while I'm at it."

"Cool." Teek smiled and then winced.

"Let me get you some acetaminophen and then you can go back to class."

"Thanks."

She retrieved two pills and handed him the pills with a

glass of water. Teek took them and Nurse Rodriguez walked him to the door. Upon opening it, he found Mary waiting there for him.

"You waited for me?" Teek asked.

"Well, duh," Mary replied. "I still have your bag."

Mary held up the bag. Teek grabbed it and smile-winced.

"Hang on, you two. Let me get you a pass," Nurse Rodriguez said and walked back into her office.

Teek grabbed Mary's hand. "Kinda makes getting my face broken worth it," he said.

"Hmm, maybe you hit your head harder than you thought," Mary replied, but kept holding his hand.

Nurse Rodriguez appeared with the passes and saw the two of them holding hands. She rolled her eyes. "Have you two had health class yet? Never mind, hold on," she said and disappeared back into her office. She came back holding two condoms. She handed a pass and a condom to each of them.

"Uh," Teek said, his face turning a bright shade of red. "We really don't need these yet."

Mary patted him playfully. "Teek, manners! Say thank you when someone gives you a gift that shows they care."

"Umm," Teek stuttered. "Th-thank you?"

Nurse Rodriguez pushed them out the door. "Use them if you get that far," she said and closed the door. Mary giggled, but Teek's face just got redder.

"You know, we got a hall pass," Mary said. "We could always find a supply closet and use these." She held up the condom and winked.

Teek pushed her hand down and looked around quickly.

"Mary!" Teek hissed.

"Relax, I'm just kidding," Mary said and giggled. "We'll use them when the time is right. Not in the middle of math class."

They made it just a few steps down the hallway when the earth began to shake.

What started as a mild shaking turned violent in just a couple of seconds. Since it was so close, Mary and Teek ran to the front entrance of the school and got out of the building quickly. Ceiling tiles pelted them as they traversed the fifty feet to the front doors, which were largely metal and remained intact. Around them, they could hear screams and shouts as the outer windows of the classrooms and school offices shattered under the strain. The school hadn't been built to handle earthquakes. There didn't use to be a need.

Once outside, and safely away from the building, Mary and Teek watched in awe as the town around them erupted in explosions from ruptured gas mains. They saw power lines fall and fires come to life all around them. Children and staff quickly emerged from the school behind them as the walls inside the structure began to buckle. A few people remained inside under desks as they'd been taught during drills the school board had deemed unnecessary but grudgingly allowed the schools to perform annually. The board merely echoed the sentiments of the town patriarch, Elbert Dawkins—there was little danger of serious earthquakes in Tuggville.

Dom and Mary managed to find the two of them in the chaos outside the school. The administrators and teachers tried to assemble the students outside, but many simply ran home. There was little chance of a head count and that would hamper rescue efforts for anyone trapped inside.

"What if she got out?" Teek asked them as they watched the craziness and haphazard rescue efforts of the school staff.

"Who?" Mary asked.

"Granny Bael!"

"So what?" Dom said. "That's someone else's problem. Let the adults handle it."

"What adults, Dom? My foster parents? Your uncle? The police and fire department? They're all going to be busy for the next few weeks. Look around."

"No, we're safe here. We should stay," Dom said. An aftershock shook everything and a power line fell into the street in front of the school. It sparked and made a continuous buzzing noise.

"She knew my name, Dom. She might know where I live," Teek said. "Those kids don't have anyone to protect them."

Jemma squeezed Dom's arm and he sighed. "Okay, let's run by your house, make sure everything is okay there, and then I guess we can drop by the District against my better judgment," Dom said. Jemma hugged him and Teek grabbed Mary's hand. They ran off. No one noticed them leaving except a foursome of boys in letterman jackets who casually slipped away and followed them.

Elbert Dawkins stood looking out his third story office window at the town several blocks away. He'd located the cement plant outside of town for multiple reasons. Sound and noise were one consideration, but even more important to him—

the remote location afforded few people the opportunity to casually snoop on his activities here at the plant. His home was even further from town for much the same reason. Although, he hadn't picked the location; he just inherited it from his father. Thinking of his father's demise brought a smile to his face.

Smoke began to rise from several locations across town and Elbert cocked his head in curiosity. "I think that's the grocery," he murmured. "That one there could be the school or perhaps the utilities building. This should be interesting."

The phone on his desk rang and he walked over to it casually. He pressed the intercom button. "Yes?"

"Mister Dawkins, this is Diane," came the old woman's voice. She was the day secretary for the plant.

"Continue," he replied.

"Sir, several employees, me included, would like to know if we can go check on our homes and families. We can see smoke rising in town and, well…"

"Of course, Miss Beringer. Give everyone the day off. Let Mister Wilkins know so he can set the books right. Families are so important," Elbert said even as he rolled his eyes and shook his head. Bunch of whiny babies. It was getting hard to find anyone with backbone in this town. "Oh, and better let my son know. Also, tell him I'd like to see him as soon as possible."

"Yes sir. Thank you, sir!"

Elbert cut the connection without responding to the last. He looked up as the lights flickered and the generator for the building took over. Electricity had gone down for some of the town including here. While the office building could run well on generator power, the plant would struggle to maintain any kind of production. As it was, the backup generators would do nicely maintaining their current inventory but any further production was unlikely.

He walked back to the window and glanced to the southwest of town where the District was located. He smiled. "Things may get very interesting indeed."

11

CHAOS

Howard pulled up outside Tuggville's largest grocery store. It was already engulfed in flames and the fire department had just arrived. Howard got out of his vehicle and looked for a moment at the four bags of cement in the back seat.

"Probably not enough now anyway," he said. He looked to the southwest of town where the District was located. There were no plumes of fire from that direction, but that didn't mean much in his eyes. Granny Bael could get out in this chaos and no one would realize it until it was too late.

Howard started assisting the fire department with crowd control and chatted on his car radio with dispatch. He was assigned to the fire while the remaining twenty officers were spread throughout town.

"Hey, can you call the Phalanx Insurance Agency?" Howard asked into the radio.

"Sure," dispatch replied. There was a pause for a few moments and then dispatch connected again.

"There doesn't seem to be any answer. Phone lines are down all around town."

"Okay," Howard replied. "Thanks."

He put the radio back and put his hands on the steering wheel.

"Shit, Rick. I hope you and Shanna can do something. This is fucked up."

Part of the grocery store front collapsed and everyone rushed his direction to escape the burning debris.

"Well, Cary, there goes your store. Couldn't happen to a nicer guy." Howard climbed out of his car to help corral the chaos.

The Phalanx Insurance Agency was a shambles. Most of the strip mall building had collapsed, but nothing had caught on fire. Dust rose from the debris as Rick struggled to get out from under his desk, pushing ceiling tiles, splintered wood and chunks of dry wall out of the way. In a way, the light construction helped with his escape. The materials were easier to push out of the way than they might have been in a sturdier build.

As he pushed his way out, he saw Shanna doing the same thing. They'd both been able to get under a desk. He didn't see Bridget moving anywhere in the rubble, though.

"Bridget?" Rick called. "Are you okay?"

"She's all right," Shanna replied. "She got under the desk with me. Help me dig us out."

Rick shambled over the rubble and helped pull chunks of building away from Shanna so she could fully extricate herself.

They pulled a shaken and dusty Bridget out of the safe space.

Rick glanced out at the parking lot and saw several ladies from the neighboring salons milling about in the parking lot. They seemed dusty but otherwise unharmed.

"Ladies, is everyone out of the building? Is everyone okay?" Rick shouted from his perch on the rubble.

"We're all okay, Rick," said one of the women Rick recognized as a manager from the salon to his right. He thought her name might be Evelyn. "A little bruised and dirty, but everyone's out."

As Rick helped Shanna and Bridget over the rubble, he glanced at the rest of the building. "I don't know if there are any gas lines, but it's probably safer to stay away from the building right now," he told the salon workers. He pulled Shanna and Bridget over to his SUV.

"Bridget," he said. "Shanna and I need to go check on something. It might be dangerous."

Shanna glared at Rick, but didn't say anything.

"If something happens to us, there's a life insurance policy with you as the beneficiary. You know we don't have kids. If the unthinkable happens, I want you to take that money and get as far away from Tuggville as it will take you."

"But," Bridget said. "My family is here."

"Take them with you. Now, more than ever, the safest place to be is nowhere near Tuggville. Do you understand?" Rick gripped her shoulders gently but firmly and looked her in the eyes. "Tell me you understand."

Bridget looked in his eyes with sadness and nodded.

"I understand, Mister Roman," she said.

When the teens arrived at the foster home, emergency personnel were already there. The two story building at the back of the property was swarming with firemen and police. It had partially collapsed owing to poor maintenance; it barely withstood normal weather. The magnitude of this quake was too much.

Teek saw his foster parents handcuffed and sitting on the ground next to a police car.

There were several sheets laid over small bodies in the field next to the building. A few children were being tended to by medical personnel. When Teek saw the bodies, he collapsed.

"Oh my God, was she here? Did she do this?" Teek had his head in his hands. He rocked back and forth on the ground. Mary knelt down and held him. Dom looked around and noticed the hoses on the fire trucks were still in place.

"Didn't that Granny person use fire? I don't think there's been any fire here. Just a collapsed building from the quake," Dom said.

Suddenly, Teek got to his feet. "I can't let her get the rest of them!" Teek said and bolted away from his friends.

"Aw shit," Dom swore. They all hurried after Teek.

Hidden behind the next house, Eric and his three teammates watched the scene unfold.

"Damn," said Victor, a tall blonde athletic teen. He was the one of the team's wide receivers.

"Poor people are always packed in like rats," Eric said. "Looks like the quake exterminated some vermin."

"That's not cool, man," the stockiest of the players, Darren, said and shoved Eric gently.

"It's not my problem, *man!*" Eric retorted, shoving him back.

"Those were just kids though," Victor said. "Don't you care about kids?"

"No, I don't care about poor, stinking, vermin that suck the resources from the town," Eric said. "My dad told me all about these leeches on society."

"Your dad's messed up," Darren replied.

Eric rushed Darren and caught him off guard, knocking him down. "Don't ever say anything about my dad!" Eric screamed at him.

"Chill out, dude," Darren said. "I didn't mean nothin' by it."

Eric stood over Darren with fists clenched and then took a breath. He glanced at the group they'd followed disappearing down the street. He turned and walked quickly in their direction. "Never mind, let's just go do what we came to do," Eric said.

Darren's two remaining teammates helped him up. "What is it we're doing exactly," Darren asked his two friends quietly.

"I don't know," Victor replied. "I think we're along just to keep Eric from doing something phenomenally stupid."

The last of them, another stocky guy who went by the nickname Brute laughed.

"That's a tall order and there are only three of us, man," Brute said and they all trotted off after Eric.

Rick braked and stopped the car from hitting the downed power line. He got out of the car and looked around. There was no way around the lines even if he jumped the curb. They effectively blocked the road out to the District. He looked back in the car at Shanna.

"Looks like we're walking," he said. Shanna pointed down to her heels and cocked her head at him.

"So throw your gym sneakers on and let's go," Rick said as he popped the trunk of the SUV.

Shanna sighed and looked ahead. In the distance she saw Teek running across the street and into the woods. His friends followed close after.

"Shanna," Rick said as he walked back up to the open driver's door. "You know we have to do this."

"I know," Shanna replied. She looked down at her wedding ring and smiled. "It's been a good life, hasn't it?"

"Yes," Rick said softly. She looked over at him and he smiled at her, just like he did on their wedding day. "Maybe if we get through this, we leave any more battles to the next generation?"

Shanna nodded and got out of the car.

When her feet hit the wet pavement, she stopped for a moment. It reminded her of that fateful night decades ago. She was there with the others but looking around for Larry, although she teasingly called him Lawrence when they were alone. He promised he'd be there when they'd all agreed Granny Bael had to be stopped. Her heart dropped out of her chest when she thought he'd just been a coward and too scared to show up. It wasn't until years later she learned his father had stopped him, literally locking him up to keep him from being there.

"Hey," Rick said. She looking over at him standing at the end of the SUV, shotgun in hand pointed at the ground. "I know this brings up a lot of memories."

"It's nothing," Shanna said as she looked down again. She walked around Rick and grabbed her tennis shoes and a pair of socks from the back. She sat on the bumper and pulled off her heels.

Rick smiled at her and sat down on the bumper next to her. "I know I wasn't your first choice," Rick said.

"I love you, Rick. You know that," Shanna replied.

"I know, but it wasn't always that way," Rick said. "I loved you from the first minute I saw you."

Shanna thought back to that awkward first meeting when she was sitting in the cafeteria at elementary school. Rick was tall even at that age, a full head above anyone else in class. He'd taken one look at her and didn't watch where he was going, tumbling over a bench and on top of all three Tulley brothers; they'd all wound up in a pile on the floor. He'd been so embarrassed; he didn't talk to anyone for four years. By then, she'd already kind of hooked up with Larry at a school dance. Not that fifth graders did anything serious, but she'd been smitten by Larry before Rick had really matured enough to try.

The crew had gravitated toward each other feeling like outcasts from the rest of the kids at high school. It was a common bond they shared—horrible home lives, awkward cold shoulders at school from other kids and a general caring for each others' plight in life. Shanna and Larry were a full blown item by then, dating, visiting each other's homes after school, and even running for prom king and queen. She'd even put up with the leers from Larry's father, Elbert, but kept a healthy distance from him. He was a creeptastic and chilling guy! Larry had recommended not going to his house anymore, which Shanna was only a little disappointed by. The building and grounds were huge and lush beyond anything else in Tuggville. She was grateful to not be under the creepy eye of Larry's father, though. Better out of sight and hopefully out of mind.

Abigail had really come into her own right about the time Granny Bael got out from whatever prison she'd been in before. Shanna remembered being jealous of the fair-haired, free-willed Abby. Larry never really paid her any mind, focusing solely on Shanna, but she couldn't help her jealous suspicious mind even when it seemed Abby only had eyes for Howard Tulley.

When Elbert Dawkins had shown up with Larry's Uncle Alex at the District to encase Granny's prison in concrete, she's looked in vain for Larry to be with them, but he was nowhere to be found. She simply ran off before the two elder Dawkins had reached the group of them. Rick trailed behind her and gave her a shoulder to cry on when she thought Larry betrayed them. Abigail and the Tulleys stayed behind, the boys' mourning their brother and Abby to provide Howard comfort in his time of need.

"You were always there for me, Rick," Shanna said as she

patted his leg. "Nothing could keep you from my side, so my choice was obvious when you told me how you felt."

"It wasn't Larry's fault," Rick said. "He really did love you."

"He married a mail order bride without even telling me, Rick," Shanna said. "Who does that? When push came to shove, he was a wimp. How could I love someone like that?"

"Everyone has their faults," Rick said. "I mean, it's Tuggville. When is it not crappy here?"

"It wasn't crappy the day I married you," Shanna replied.

"Except for the thunderstorm and sheltering in the basement of the courthouse," Rick said and they both laughed.

"Tuggville never disappoints in disappointing her residents," Shanna said. She finished tying her shoes and stood up. "Let's make sure Granny doesn't get any more notches in her belt, okay?" Shanna asked. She grabbed a bag from next to the spare tire and skipped around to the front of the SUV. Rick slammed the trunk shut and joined her. They began the long walk to the District.

12
A CRACK IN TIME

Teek arrived at the spot in the forest they'd approached from before and leaned against a tree to catch his breath. The quake had collapsed all the warehouses across their previous path. A few minutes passed before the others caught up and rested as well. Jemma surveyed the damage and shook her head.

"We're not going in that way again," she said. She turned to the others. "Go in the front like Dom's uncle?"

"We'll just go in on the other side of this collapsed building. I scouted it days ago and it should be clear," Teek said. He pushed himself off the tree and walked further into the forest. The others followed him and pushed their way through the slightly thicker foliage.

Far behind them at the edge of the forest, Eric's companions grabbed his shoulder to stop him from going in.

"What?" Eric asked.

"Dude, this is the District," Victor said.

"So," Eric began as he turned to go in.

Victor grabbed his shoulder again. "People go in there, they don't come out."

"That's the plan, for Dom to not come out," Eric said.

"Seriously, dude?" Darren asked. "Why you so hot to hurt Dom anyway?"

"Because he's a big, fucking dumb nigger that doesn't know his place," Eric said.

"No, man," Victor said. "That's racist as fuck."

"You want them taking your money, taking your business, taking your women?" Eric said as he got up in Victor's face.

"Women?" Darren asked, laughing. "Is this about Jemma? Dude, she ain't gonna want you if you kill Dom. How fucking stupid is that?"

"We need to put them in their place!" Eric shouted.

The three teammates backed away with their hands up. "This ain't the fifties, bro," Brute said. "That's not how it is anymore."

"You're fucking idiots!" Eric screamed. "My dad told me there'd be idiots I'd have to leave behind. I guess you're them."

"Your dad's messed up your head, man," Victor replied. He shook his head.

"Niggers will be fucking your slut ass mom next," Eric sneered.

"That's it dude, we're done." Victor turned and walked away, flipping Eric the finger. Darren and Brute just shook their heads and turned their backs on Eric.

"Teammates stick together!" Eric shouted at them.

"Dom's your fucking teammate, asshole," Victor shouted back over his shoulder.

"Fuck you!" Eric shouted. He turned around and ran into the forest.

As they walked away, Darren turned to Brute. "Think we should warn Dom?"

"Bro, if Eric's dumb enough to go one on one against Dom, he deserves the butt kicking he's about to get," Brute said. "Maybe we hazed Dom too much, gave Eric the wrong idea about us."

"Eric gets the wrong idea from his dad," Victor said. "Ain't got nothing to do with us. But we probably should lay off Dom. Eric's racist rant left a bad taste in my mouth. We don't need that kind of rep."

Teek led the group to the other side of the collapsed building. The concrete here was just as broken up and challenging as the other side, but it didn't have parts of building strewn all across it.

"Come on," Teek said as he deftly maneuvered over the broken terrain.

"Teek," Mary called. "I don't mean to be mean, but... do you have a plan?"

Teek stopped in his tracks and blinked.

"We... umm," Teek said. He scratched his head. "We kill it?"

"Kill what?" Jemma asked.

"You know," Teek said as he started moving again. "The Granny witch thing."

"You don't even know what we're going to find, but if it's loose, you want to kill it?" Jemma leaped across a gap in the concrete. She felt the first sprinkles of rain on her face and looked up, noticing dark clouds forming.

"We'll just see what has happened. If anything has gotten out that looks dangerous, we'll tell Dom's uncle," Teek replied as he reached the end of the building and stopped.

"He's not gonna be happy to hear from us," Dom said. "Besides, I think he might be a little busy with the disaster happening in town."

They all joined Teek at the edge of the building and looked at the concrete mound in the middle of the lot. There were significant cracks on this side. Bits of daylight streamed through the openings.

Teek turned to his friends. "Look, this thing, whatever it is, knows my name. Who knows what else it knows about me and my foster brothers and sisters? I can't rest until I know for certain what it is and see if we can stop it from hurting anyone."

Mary grabbed his hand and squeezed it.

There was a sound of rubble shifting on the other side of the building. They all looked, but didn't see anything moving.

"Okay," Dom said. "Let's see what this thing is. Hopefully it's just a raccoon or something."

"That talks?" Teek asked. He shook his head and turned around. "I don't know about you sometimes, Dom."

"Well," Jemma began as they all started toward the sarcophagus. "I wouldn't put it past the bullies at school to set up a speaker and just call out your name to scare you.

Scare us.”

"They're mean, but I don't think they're that clever," Teek replied. "When I turn eighteen, I'm leaving Tuggville and those idiots behind. If the quarry wasn't closed, I'd say they'll wind up beating rocks together for a living."

Mary snickered and Teek smiled. Then they all laughed. When they reached the edge of the cement structure, it was clear the quake had done a lot of damage to it. Teek peered through one of the holes and saw the silhouette of a barrel in the middle of the hollow building. He also noticed the break on the other side that he poked yesterday was big enough to walk through.

"Well," Teek said. "We're finally going to find out what's in here."

He stood up and walked around to the other side. Everyone joined him and they just stood there looking at the opening. Inside, they could see some rubble on the floor surrounding a thick line of salt that appeared to be drawn around a barrel in the center of the room. There was something that looked like a big pile of charcoal sitting against the barrel.

"It's not talking now," Dom said. "Maybe the earthquake smashed the hidden speakers."

A scraping sound made them all jump. It came from one of the buildings. The light mist from the skies became a sprinkle.

"These buildings are all falling down," Dom said. "Nothing to worry about."

"I wasn't worried," Jemma said. They all chuckled nervously.

"Okay," Teek said. "You all ready?"

Mary grabbed Teek's arm. "Are you sure?" she asked.

Teek could see the concern in her eyes and it gave him strength. He patted her on the hand. "Let's do this," Teek said and he stepped forward into the opening.

The thick slab of cement that had fallen inward was firm and solid, but the edges were lined with steel bars that had rusted through. All around were chunks of concrete of various sizes.

"Watch your step," Teek said.

The others followed Teek, with Dom to the rear of them. Teek walked around to the other side, observing the salt circle around the barrel appeared unbroken. He wondered how long that would last.

"Is that a body?" Mary asked, peering at the charred pile resting against the barrel. As if in response to her question, the charred globe on top tumbled off the body revealing a fully charred human skull. Everyone screamed as the skull fell and came to rest just inside the circle at Mary's feet.

"Poor Edward," an old woman's voice creaked. It seemed to come from all around them. "He tried to set me free, but his friends burned him alive."

"Uncle Edward?" Dom blurted out and then slapped his hands over his mouth.

"Yes, Dominique Tulley," the voice answered. "Don't you think the ones who did this should be punished for their crimes?"

"She lies," Mary said. "Your uncle Howard wouldn't do this to his own brother."

"Ah, Mary Verdoon, niece of Crazy Abby Partridge. It's a shame your aunt spread her legs to invite evil into her. She's a real slut for evil. Very unbecoming of a young lady."

"What the hell are you talking about?" Mary shot back. "You're the evil one!"

"Am I? Must make you excited then since you carry the same bloodline as your aunt."

"Shut the fuck up," Mary said.

"So ladylike," the old voice cackled. "I can guess where you got it from. Certainly not from my side."

"Leave her alone!" Teek shouted at the barrel.

"Poor little Teek Martin," the voice crooned. "Took the name of his dead mother because he doesn't know who his father is. Do you want to know, little Teek? I'll bet your half sister would like to know."

"You're sick!" Teek said.

"Evil begets evil, little Teek," the voice replied. "You've got the taint of it, but Jemma, you're brimming with evil."

"I've heard enough, let's go. Let this thing rot in its tomb," Dom said.

Eric suddenly rushed in from behind Dom, swinging a piece of rebar at his head. "Die," Eric shouted, "you piece of shit nig—" but he was cut off as Dom deflected it, knocking Eric off balance. He tumbled forward into the charred remains of Edward Tulley and caught himself on the barrel.

Everyone's eyes went wide as Eric floated up into the air, impaled on a rod of fire emanating from the barrel. The fire quickly engulfed Eric. He writhed and screamed in the air as he burned.

"Stupid kid," Rick said from the opening. He raised his shotgun and aimed at the rod of fire, letting loose a spray of salted buck shot. The burning rod retracted and Eric's burning body fell to the ground. He lay motionless.

"You other kids get out," Rick shouted. "We'll take it from here."

Rick stepped into the room and Shanna walked in behind him. The kids squeezed past them, exiting the sarcophagus. They stopped outside and watched as Shanna raised a bag of salt and some candles.

"We've come to finish what Abby started," Shanna said.

"This ends tonight," Rick said.

"Oh, has Crazy Abby come up with a way to get rid of me for good?" the voice responded. "I'm shaking with fear." The old lady cackled and it made the kids outside shiver. The rain that was soaking them to the bone didn't help.

Shanna pulled a piece of paper from a bag.

"You're finished Granny Bael," Rick said.

"Oh, I like that nickname. I think I'll keep it," the voice responded. "The funny thing is how you think you're in control."

With that, the ground shook and a chunk of cement fell from the ceiling, striking Rick on the back of the head. He fell forward and two claws of fire and brimstone grabbed him and twirled him around violently, causing Rick to pull the trigger of the shotgun involuntarily. The blast hit Shanna in the chest and propelled her back out of the opening of the sarcophagus. As she traveled through, her head struck one of the edges of the remaining rebar with a loud crack, peeling her skull open on the right side and exposing a mess of blood and bone. She landed on her back and howled in pain.

The kids all jumped back. Rick screamed in agony from within the sarcophagus which glowed orange as he burned alive. The sickly smell of burnt human flesh intensified.

Shanna, somehow still conscious, turned her head to look at the kids, the bloody flap of her skull flopping over onto the right side of her face. "Run!" she shouted at them.

They turned tail and ran for the fence at the front of the compound.

Shanna turned her face back to the sky as rain and blood poured down her face. "Shit," she said before she closed her eyes and fell silent.

13
THE CIRCLE

Tuggville only had one police station right in the middle of town. With the electricity and phones down, the kids didn't have many options. Their panicked run turned into a walk and then a wet slog as they trudged their way to the middle of town. The rain finally stopped just as they reached their destination.

Dom was first through the front door of the station. He approached the front desk lit up only by the internal emergency lights and the scant sunlight filtering in through the sparse windows.

The sergeant sitting there looked up and smiled. "Hey, Dom! What brings you soaking wet rats here in the middle of a town wide disaster?" the lanky sergeant asked with a wink.

"I'm really sorry about this, but I need to talk to my uncle. It's urgent."

The sergeant laughed, thinking it was a joke. When Dom didn't join in, the sergeant sighed.

"Well, Officer Tulley isn't here. Power's out across town,

phones are down and, last I heard, your uncle was providing support to the firemen at the grocery store."

"Oh," Jemma said. "Eric's dad!"

"Now, now. He's just reported as missing. Dom, I know you guys on the football team are close, but you can't tell Eric anything. We'll send an officer to his home when we confirm. Poor kid had it rough enough with a dad like Cary Deering shoving all that crap into his head. He's going to be messed up for a while. Promise me you won't tell him," the sergeant said and pointed his finger at Dom.

"I promise none of us will tell Eric anything," Dom said solemnly. "You think you can give us a ride?"

"I can't leave my post and everyone else is out. It's a pretty messed up day. Sorry, kid."

"That's okay, thank you," Dom said and he led the others out of the station.

"Why didn't you tell him about Eric?" Jemma asked.

"Tell him a fire demon killed Eric and two other people in the District where nobody is supposed to go? No thanks. I'll take my chances with my uncle."

Teek started shaking and stopped walking.

Mary immediately stopped. "Teek?" She asked. Dom and Jemma stopped too.

"It's just a lot, ya know?" Teek blinked his eyes rapidly but the tears started to fall. Mary hugged him tight.

"You're strong, Teek," Mary said. "You can get through this. You're stronger than anyone else I know."

Dom leaned over to whisper in Jemma's ear. "They've totally been doing it," Dom said.

Jemma turned to Dom and smiled. "You really shouldn't be joking about what we should be doing as well," Jemma said.

Dom's jaw hung open. He totally forgot about Teek and Mary for a moment. "Well, I didn't know you felt that way too," Dom said.

"I know, because boys are thick-headed and clueless sometimes," Jemma said.

"Well," Dom started to object and then nodded. "Yeah, yeah we are." Dom took her hand and she smiled at him. He touched her cheek gently. "What about your dad?" Dom asked.

"You're not going to be making out with him," Jemma said with a smirk.

"True dat," Dom said and pulled her close for a deep kiss. Years of attraction and unrequited desire erupted between them through some passionate kissing. They forgot about everything around them.

"Hey," Teek said. "Get a room! We got places to be, ya know?"

Dom and Jemma separated and looked at Mary and Teek staring at them with arms folded. Teek started walking toward the grocery store, plainly marked by the column of smoke rising in the distance.

"Time and a place, guys," Mary said as she walked by them. She turned her head and winked. Then Mary rushed to catch up with Teek and held his hand as they continued to walk. Dom and Jemma laughed as they ran to catch up with them.

Howard took the wet and dirty raincoat off and shook it out, then tossed it into the back of his patrol car. He popped open a bottle of water and rinsed off his hands and face, removing much of the soot that had gotten caked on during the fire. He tipped his head back and rinsed his eyes briefly as best as he could; they burned fiercely from the smoke.

Behind Howard, the fire department continued to douse the grocery store with water to mop up the hot spots, but the fire had largely gone out. Howard glanced at them and then saw the lone detective in the department pull up. The detective got out of his car and walked over to Howard.

"Officer Tulley," he said as he approached. "What's the situation?"

"Hey, Bill," Howard replied. "I don't know if it's cool enough to get to, but the firemen tell me there's a body in the office, looks like he was holding a fire extinguisher. Didn't have enough sense to get out of the burning building, I guess. They suspect it's the owner."

"Cary Deering," Bill replied. "Well, that's going to put a hurt on the local grocery supply. Not sure we'll miss the old bastard for anything else."

"I think he's got a kid," Howard said.

Bill nodded. "Eric. He's on the football team. Kicker, I think. Trust me, with Cary out of his life, he'll probably be the better for it." Bill started walking toward the grocery store. "I've got a call into the state police for help with the scene. You can go on to whatever they need you for next. I got this."

"Thanks, Bill," Howard said as he sat down in his car and

grabbed the radio. He was about to check in when he saw the kids in the rearview mirror. "Well, what the heck are they doing here?"

He set the radio down and got out of the car. "Dom, ain't you and your friends supposed to be in school or home?" Howard was jovial but concerned. He knew school probably sent them home anyway shortly after the devastating quake.

Dom sped up a little and everyone matched his speed. He stopped when he reached Howard.

"We got a problem," Dom said. "She's out."

"Who's out? One of you missing a dog or something?"

"Granny Bael," Dom said.

Howard felt goose bumps break out all over him. "How do you know about Granny Bael," Howard said.

"It doesn't matter," Dom said. "She killed Eric and some guy who showed up with a shotgun and a redheaded lady with some salt and candles."

Howard looked over at the grocery store. "Eric," he said. It took a moment for him to process who the other two people were. He looked angrily at Dom. "Rick and Shanna?! Dammit! What the hell were you guys doing there?"

"I'm sorry," Dom replied sheepishly.

"Was the circle broken?" Howard asked.

"Circle, you mean the building?" Dom scratched his head.

"No, on the ground!" Howard yelled. "Was it broken?"

"You mean the salt," Mary asked.

"Yes, the salt circle. Was it broken?"

"Well, when we went inside—" Mary started.

"You went inside?!" Howard shouted. Mary jumped and

stepped back. Howard closed his eyes and took a deep breath. "I'm sorry. It sounds like some friends of mine may have been hurt and I'm a little upset. I apologize. Go on."

"I walked all around and the circle seemed intact. Then Eric attacked Dom and fell onto the barrel in the center."

"Did he disturb the circle?" Howard asked.

"I'm not sure. Then the guy with the gun showed up and shot the burning thing that was stabbing Eric. And then he—" Mary stopped. The words stuck in her throat. She could see the horror in her mind, but the words wouldn't come out. The picture of Eric's charred corpse hitting the ground at Dom's feet was something she'd suppressed until just then. Now she couldn't get it out of her mind. The smell. The awful smell!

Mary turned away from them and threw up on the ground. They all looked like they would be sick. It came back to them all at once. They hadn't processed it before; they just let the adrenaline drive them on. A fellow student had burned to death in front of them. There's no way that trauma would lay hidden forever.

Howard looked around at these kids and the memory came flooding back to him. He and his two brothers, Edward and Troy had joined forces with Abigail, Rick and Shanna to put Granny Bael down for good. But Granny somehow knew how to get under everyone's skin. She ticked Edward off and he lost control, jumping into the circle and stabbing at Granny's trapped flesh within the barrel as she continued to taunt him. Then the fire just reached up and enveloped him as Abigail tearfully completed the incantation to lock Granny Bael in the barrel.

Even as they backed away, Granny Bael continued. She badgered him and Troy about abandoning their brother to die. Cowards, she'd called them. As Edward's corpse slumped against the barrel, smoking and crackling, Howard had to grab his brother's arm to stop him from going at her as well. Troy buried that night deep inside, but eventually it resurfaced and he began to drink. He never stopped drinking. Howard theorized he was probably sitting in a bar somewhere right now with his hand wrapped around a whiskey bottle. He preferred a booth so if he passed out he wouldn't hit the floor. Howard knew their trauma, but he needed answers.

"I know this is difficult for you right now, but I need to know if that salt circle was broken," Howard said calmly.

"The guy with the gun burned up like Eric, I guess," Jemma choked out. "He shot the woman with the salt and candles for some reason. It might've been an accident. She told us to run before she... I think she died. We didn't stick around to find out."

Howard nodded. "Shanna was good people. She wanted to keep you kids safe. Honorable to the end," Howard said as he slumped against the patrol car. He looked at the ground for a long time. They probably wouldn't have been there at all if he hadn't told them. His friends were dead because of him. Just like Edward. He never would've gone to dig up that demon bitch without Howard's prodding. They couldn't die in vain.

His thoughts drifted back to the old mill. He took the whole gang there, the Latchkey Losers they called themselves. They were all there to search for the remains of

Granny Balsom. Howard had heard the tale from Murphy, the head mechanic at the repair shop. Old Granny Balsom, burned at the stake and then interred under the old mill. Old man Dawkins had told the whole mob that this was the only way to keep her soul trapped forever. They'd bought into his explanations hook, line and sinker.

Wait, no. Someone else had told them where she was. Someone in the library slipped Howard a note after he heard the tale from Murphy. Murphy didn't know where she was buried. It didn't matter to them where they got the information, though. Once they had the clue to her whereabouts, there wasn't much that could stop them from their macabre obsession.

The Latchkey Losers crew had been there a dozen times before, the last six times with shovels. They'd never found anything. But this night, the first shovelful had turned up some black, ashy substance. It was Edward working the shovel this particular night and he'd given out a shout and everyone had come running to see what he'd found. The soot eventually gave way to a finger bone. That was enough for all of them. They ran from the old mill and never returned.

But the next night, she rose from the ground and the old mill went up in flames. As the nights progressed deeper into October, more buildings burned and eventually, Granny Balsom made her first appearance on the outskirts of town, killing an old farmer and his wife. The following night, old man Dawkins was gathering people to hunt her down again when she appeared where they were gathered in the town square, killing most of them including old man Dawkins. They found the bodies at dawn the next day and that was the day the little notebook had turned up in Abigail's locker at the high school. It was wrapped in a note that told them to look on a certain page to defeat Granny Balsom.

They never found out where the book came from, but it had everything they needed in it to trap Granny Balsom at the District that night.

Howard stood up and took a deep breath. "Get in the car. We're going to Dawkins Cement," Howard said.

"Why?" Jemma asked.

"Your dad's going to help like he didn't twenty years ago," Howard said and got in the car.

14
DEVILS

Howard pulled up next to the lineman working on a downed power line. He rolled the window down. "Hey, I need to talk to your supervisor," Howard said.

Dom sat in the front seat next to his uncle. He stared at the dashboard, still processing the horrors of the day. Jemma watched from the back seat, wishing she could hold his hand even as the events raced through her own mind.

Another man walked up and nodded his head at Howard. "What can I do for you," he looked in the car and saw the kids. "Officer Tulley?"

"Hey Jim, I need Occidental cleared. We've got an emergency over that way and I need to get vehicles through," Howard said.

"We've got the whole town without power, even the hospital. I'm working as fast as I can."

"Jim, I need this favor like I've never needed another favor. The town's survival depends on it more than power restoration will," Howard said sternly.

Jim raised his eyebrows. "All right, Howard. We just got this cleared. I'll make Occidental the next stop." Jim looked in the car at the kids again. "Hope everything turns out all right."

"Well, if it doesn't, you'll know soon enough. So will everyone in town."

"Fair enough," Jim said. He turned around and shouted out orders to his crew.

Howard rolled up the window and they sped off.

Jemma looked at Howard in the rearview mirror. "What did you mean my dad didn't help last time?" Jemma asked.

Howard looked at her in the rearview and sighed. "It wasn't meant to be a dig on your dad, but he wasn't there when the rest of us faced Granny down. Your grandfather saw to that."

Jemma looked out the window. She had pleasant memories of her grandmother and even her mom before she started drinking. Her dad was always stern and not much fun at all. Her grandfather was always distant. She had no real positive memories, just formal introductions and appearances at events. She never spent time with him growing up. "What happened?"

"He never told you? No, I guess he wouldn't. None of us really know much." Howard shook his head. "Maybe we better start at the beginning. Fifty years ago, there was a hideous set of murders. The entire Balsom family was slaughtered in their home."

"Yeah, yeah, the legend of Granny Bael. We've already heard it," Jemma said.

"Have you? Rumors had it your grandfather was up to some shady doings and the elder Elwin was always covering for him," Howard said. "Did you hear about that?"

"No, what does it matter?"

"Larry, your dad, was always hounded by those rumors. When he was free to roam and hang out with us, we talked a lot about how cruel your grandfather was to him, the rest of the family, his employees. I don't think anyone ever escaped his wrath. Larry did everything he could to never be home when his dad was. Until we accidentally released Granny, he had his freedom. When everything started going to hell, your grandfather confined him to home under the thumb of a personal security team."

"That's crazy!" Jemma retorted. "Do you know how expensive that would be?"

"That does sound a little outrageous, Uncle," Dom added.

"Do…" Howard looked at Dom and then at all the kids in the rearview mirror. "Do you know how rich Elbert Dawkins is?"

"He owns the cement company," Jemma said. "Does cement make you that rich?"

The kids laughed.

"The cement company is where you can most often find him," Howard replied. "But he owns this town. Utilities, all the buildings and even the damn school are owned by him. That's why no one owns a house here—they're all owned by Elbert Dawkins. He runs the town council. He's blocked cell towers and internet; hell, I figure he would've blocked phones if they hadn't already been here."

"My dad didn't tell me any of this," Jemma said. She looked around at her friends. "Did you guys know this?"

"We've been to your house; we know you're not rich. I didn't know all that stuff about your grandfather," Mary said. "We were just told to stay away from him. He could ruin your life."

"That's what my mom told me, but I thought that was just the drinking talking," Jemma said.

"What does he do exactly?" Teek asked.

"I'm not sure," Howard said. "Most of this is just rumors and gossip. Don't cross Elbert Dawkins or you could be 'disappeared.' I've seen whole families disappear, but as far as I know they just moved away. I've tried looking into it, but the chief told me to leave it alone. Tuggville is a town full of secrets."

They turned a corner and the cement plant loomed up ahead. The towering silos and tops of conveyer belts towered over the tree line. A tall fence behind a row of trees marked the large facility's outer boundaries. The Dawkins Concrete signs on the fence were simple and utilitarian.

The rain stopped and steam rose from the road as the sun came out. The sound of the tires on the wet road reverberated through the patrol car. They pulled up into the parking lot and Howard shut off the car and sighed.

"You kids can stay in here if you want," Howard said. "I just need to speak with Larry and get him on board."

The kids looked at each other.

"I think we'd all like to get some fresh air," Jemma said.

"Suit yourself," Howard replied and got out. He walked to

the receiving office as Larry Dawkins stepped out. Larry was a stocky man with black hair which peeked out in an unruly fashion from under a safety helmet. Larry's face constricted into a scowl when he saw Jemma exit the patrol car.

"What the hell have you done now, Jemma?" Larry shouted across the parking lot as his face reddened. Howard intercepted him before he could complete his storming march to his daughter.

"Hey, Larry. Relax. They're not in any trouble," Howard said as he set his hand on Larry's shoulder.

"Then what the hell are they doing showing up here in a police car in the middle of a school day, Howard?" Larry retorted, though the color in his face was returning to normal.

"They've been a witness to some trouble," Howard said. "We need to shore up the sarcophagus in the District."

Larry rolled his eyes. "I'm not donating company resources because of a fairy tale," Larry said. He looked at the kids. "Did they put you up to this?" He looked at the kids as his face got red again. "Pranking law officers is a crime, idiots!"

"It's good intel, Larry. Three people are dead. Rick and Shanna," Howard said.

It was like a light bulb turned off in Larry's face. The color drained out and his jaw hung open. "No," Larry shook his head and turned away. "That can't be. She can't be," his voice cracked.

From the shadows of the office building just inside the entrance, a figure emerged. Jemma recognized her grandfather immediately; it was as if he'd stepped out of a picture from the last time she'd seen him at her twelfth birthday party. He was tall and wore a pressed suit. His wrinkled face betrayed his age, but the way he held himself showed that age hadn't affected him otherwise. His gray hair was perfectly arranged on his head. He walked calmly but with purpose toward Larry.

"Pull yourself together, Lawrence. You're an embarrassment," Elbert said.

Larry took in a deep breath and stood up straight.

"I've got this handled father, they were just leaving," Larry said. He turned back to Howard. "I'm afraid we cannot spare those resources at this time."

"Nonsense, Lawrence," Elbert said as he stopped in front of Larry. "Granny Bael is not a danger to be toyed with. You'll give them what they need and personally assist them with the forms and pouring."

"Father," Larry replied. "This is a waste of resources. We can't afford them. We have calls coming in from all over town with orders for repairs and you let everyone go for the day."

Elbert struck Larry across the face forcefully. Larry stumbled for a moment. Jemma and Mary gasped.

"Don't you dare defy me!" Elbert said with a sudden wrath that made everyone jump. He closed on Larry and grabbed his shirt. "You try my patience, boy, and you will outlive your usefulness to me!"

Howard stepped forward with his hands up. "Hey, thank you for the cement, Mister Dawkins. It's much appreciated," Howard said.

Elbert turned and his face was contorted with rage. It quickly turned into a smile and he loosened his grip on

Larry's shirt. "Anything to help, Officer Tulley," Elbert said with a graceful smile. He let go of Larry's shirt. "Lawrence will help you with whatever you need to lock that nuisance away for good." He straightened Larry's shirt for him as Larry took a deep breath to recover his wits. "Spare no expense, Lawrence. Get it done quickly. Pretend you're competent," Elbert said and patted him on the arm. He turned to Howard. "Take Officer Tulley and these two young men to assist you. I know we're short staffed due to the earthquake."

Larry nodded walked into the plant. He turned and waved at Howard and the boys to follow him. Officer Tulley, Dom and Teek followed Larry into the plant.

Elbert watched them go. When they were out of sight, he turned and walked to Jemma and Mary. He looked them up and down, assessing them with a leer.

"Grandfather?" Jemma asked, her voice quivering with discomfort.

Elbert held up his hand and smiled. "Don't speak," Elbert said. "Women should listen and obey, but never speak unless given permission."

Jemma and Mary mirrored each other with a drop of their jaw.

"You have both grown into beautiful, healthy, and delightful young women. So fair and ethereal," Elbert said calmly. "You are both aware of the danger of crossing me. What would happen to both you and your families would be tragic, deadly even, if you were to not listen to my instructions and follow them to every minute detail. You'll speak of this to no one lest they find themselves pitched off the side of the quarry, their lifeless bodies twisting in the wind before they strike the water, sinking to the bottom. Am I understood?"

"Yes sir," Jemma said.

Elbert turned to Mary and narrowed his eyes at her hesitance.

Mary swallowed hard before replying. "Yes sir," Mary said.

Elbert smiled again. "Jemma, you're so like your mother. That lovely olive skin, bright eyes, so youthful and... perky. What a fantastic purchase she was. And Mary, you're the spitting image of your aunt Abigail when she was your age. Delightful. Yes, she was so delightful then. That golden hair is simply mesmerizing."

The girls looked at each other briefly, failing miserably to hide the disgust they felt for Elbert's observations. He returned his dreadful leer to Jemma and she nearly vomited right then.

"Your grandmother, may she rest, was so insistent on having children even though she was barren. I thought the adoption of your father and your two aunts, may they rest, was a waste of time and money, but seeing as how it has led to such a fine specimen, perhaps it wasn't such a waste after all."

The more disgusted they seemed, the broader Elbert's smile became. Then, like flicking a light switch, he transformed to a businesslike demeanor, passionless and purely authoritarian. "You will both be at my estate on Saturday. Wear whatever you like; you'll be changing into outfits I've picked out for both of you. Four PM sharp. Understood?"

"But... you're my grandfather," Jemma whispered.

"I'm much more than that, Jemma. Now, think for a moment. If I'm comfortable committing murder, torture and ordering the same done on a whim, do you really think incest or rape are things I wouldn't commit with relish and impunity? Besides, your soul was doomed when you were born. There's no way to undo that, so you might as well embrace the dark side. I'll see you ladies this weekend. Not a word," Elbert finished. He smiled and turned away from them.

The girls watched him go. "He can't be serious," Mary said.

Elbert turned on a dime and cocked his head. "Should I provide an example with one of your friends? Perhaps the one they call Teek?" he asked with the same charming smile. The girls shivered.

"No," Mary said, her face suddenly pale. "We'll be there."

"Excellent. It would be a shame to let him go in such a manner. He could still be of use."

Elbert turned back around and walked away with a giddy bounce in his step.

15

SCHOOLED

Jemma and Mary leaned against the patrol car. They just stared at the ground silently. The sun was shining, but their skin was covered with goose bumps. Whether it was the wet clothing they were still in or the demands of Elbert Dawkins, neither of them felt well.

Howard returned with the boys. He saw the girls standing motionless against his car, their faces void of emotion like they were in a trance, and slowed down.

"Things didn't go so well with Elbert? He give you a talking to for messing with something you shouldn't?" Howard's teasing tone fell flat when Jemma looked up and her lips quivered for a moment.

"Something like that," Jemma replied. "We ready to go or what?"

"Yeah," Howard said. "We—" The girls didn't wait for him to finish and got in the patrol car. "—are going to meet your dad there," Howard finished and looked at Dom and Teek.

They just shrugged their shoulders.

"Uh, girls got emotional stuff sometimes," Teek said and ran around to the other side of the car.

Howard shook his head and got in. When everyone was ready, he backed the car up. In the rearview mirror, he saw a plume of smoke from the cement truck's exhaust stacks.

"Larry's on the move," Howard said and they drove out of the parking lot.

Teek tried to hold Mary's hand but she pulled it away and set it in her lap. "What's wrong?" Teek whispered.

"Just leave her alone!" Jemma screamed causing Howard to swerve slightly.

"Jemma?" Dom asked.

"Leave us both alone," Jemma said and then looked out the window.

"Man," Howard muttered. "I ain't never havin' daughters."

Dom raised his eyebrows at his uncle, but didn't say anything.

Howard looked up in the sky and sighed. "We need to get this moving. Granny will be more powerful at night."

"Why is that?" Dom asked.

"I don't know. It just always seemed safer during the day. She moves through the darkness, seems to draw power from it. She avoids the daylight."

"So you guys locked her away in total darkness for twenty years?" Dom asked.

Howard looked at his nephew and gave a half-smile. "Yeah, well, when you put it like that, I guess that wasn't such a great idea, but it's not like we had a lot of alternatives."

"You couldn't put that barrel out in the sunlight?" Dom asked.

"Well, that would weaken her theoretically, but to what end? We couldn't destroy her."

"What about banishing her to another, like, dimensional plane or something?" Teek asked.

"Oh, you know how to do that?" Howard asked. Teek shook his head. "Yeah, well, neither did we."

Teek put his hand on Mary's again, but she pulled it away. Mary winced as if in pain at what she'd done. The tears snuck out of her eyes, but she quickly wiped them away. Teek looked out the window and tried to hide his face from the others.

"Hmm," Howard mused. "Maybe Abby has found some way to do that, though. Lord knows she's had years to research it squirreled away in that cottage."

The last part Howard said with a soft sadness. The years had taken so much away from all of them. "Fucking Tuggville," Howard muttered.

Larry pulled up next to Howard's patrol car. Everyone was out of the car pushing the gate aside. Larry climbed down from the cab and walked over to the opening they were creating. The concrete was pretty solid in most places, but there were a few spots that had crumbled away.

"Howard," Larry called out. Howard ran over to him and Larry pointed at the spots. "These are going to be a problem. We'll need to get some lumber or fill from these buildings. We don't want the truck getting bogged down before we're close to the sarcophagus or we'll be running cement around in wheelbarrows all night."

"You know," Howard said. "We probably should make sure the circle is intact. Otherwise, this is pointless."

"Fine," Larry said and rolled his eyes. The kids joined them as they moved forward to the sarcophagus. As they got closer, they spotted Shanna lying where she'd fallen earlier, eyes open staring at the sky. A large pool of blood spread out beneath her back. Larry stopped and just stared at her for a moment.

"Damn," he whispered.

Howard poked his head into the sarcophagus and then went in. He took a quick trip around the barrel and salt circle, stepping carefully over Eric's burned and mutilated corpse. He paused to look at the bodies inside the circle near the barrel. One was freshly burned; that had to be Rick, Howard surmised. The other pile of burned material must be Edward. The sound of Edward screaming as he was skewered and burned alive by Granny Bael all those years ago thundered in Howard's head. He turned away from the corpses and looked at the opening. He retched a little but choked it down. He stepped quickly to the exit.

As Howard came back out of the sarcophagus, he rubbed his hands together and smiled grimly.

"Okay, it stinks like burned corpses in there, but it looks like Shanna was able to get the salt reinforced and got a couple candles lit. Maybe she got that incantation off before she died after all." Howard stepped next to Larry. "Where you want to start?"

"She was dead when we left," Jemma said. "How could she light the candles?"

"You *think* she was dead. She was still speaking right? She rushed you guys off so she could take care of things, I'm sure. Before she, you know…" Howard waved his hands at Shanna's body.

"We can't leave her like this," Larry said. "She deserves better than being buried in a nameless, concrete tomb."

"Sure." Howard nodded. "We'll just drag her off to the side."

"No, she deserves a decent burial. She should be taken to the mortuary." Larry rubbed his face in his hands. Howard looked at Eric's body in the sarcophagus and Rick's burned corpse stuck to the barrel.

"Right, she deserves better," Howard said. "Look, I've got an emergency blanket in the back of my patrol car. I can put down the seat and we can get her put in there. I'll drive her to Dolway's."

Larry nodded. The mortuary was on the other side of town, but Howard could likely get there faster in an emergency vehicle than a hearse could make it here. Provided the roads were cleared at this point, which was anything but guaranteed.

"Okay, kids! I guess we get to learn how to move a dead body today. You're welcome!" Howard said and sprinted back to his car. The kids followed close behind.

Larry stood there just looking at Shanna. "How did it go so wrong, Shanna? Meant to be together, destined to be apart."

Larry's memories tossed him back into the locked safe room in the middle of the building, small and cramped. The room had supplies and a video monitor that cycled between several views of the estate including the hallway outside the safe room. There was a bed, chair and desk with books, notebook and a few pencils in a cup. A small door led to a tiny lavatory that could be reached without leaving the safe room.

"Your freedom is done," Elbert had said to him. "Get used to the room. You'll be here a while."

"My friends are counting on me!" Larry had screamed at his father and tried to shove him aside. Two well muscled, armed men grabbed Larry and tossed him back on the lone bed in the safe room.

"Your friends released Granny Balsom upon an unsuspecting town. You are no longer to socialize with such reckless vermin."

For hours afterward, Larry beat upon the door leading out until his hands were raw and bleeding. He was stuck inside the room for three days before he got a single visitor. His father.

"I want to see Shanna!" Larry shouted at his father when he opened the door.

"Isn't that the red-haired lass fucking Rick Roman? That is his name, right?"

"What?"

"Tall, lanky fellow that hung out with you and stabbed you in the back the moment you let your guard down. Rick Roman, right?"

Larry collapsed on the bed and wouldn't respond for the rest of the day. It was weeks before he got to walk the grounds again and always under the guard of the two men who shadowed him constantly. His father showed him a wedding announcement for Rick and Shanna a few years later, right before he introduced Larry to Diedre. He claimed Diedre was a visiting foreign exchange student; Diedre was instructed to play along. Larry didn't learn until later that Diedre had no family back in China from where she had been 'imported.'

None of this was Diedre's fault, but Larry felt bitter about it all the same. When things got hard at work, especially with his father, he sometimes took his frustrations out on the poor woman. She never raised her voice until she hit the postpartum depression after David was born. The therapy had only made things worse and then the drinking started—it was a form of self medication he was powerless to stop. He felt guilty like he was partly responsible and maybe he was. He didn't know. Everything in his life felt so out of his control.

His eyes returned to Shanna's face. The flap of bloody skin hanging over her nose caused him to turn away, tears in his eyes.

When the kids and Howard got back with the blanket, Howard spread it out a few steps away from the blood pool. "Okay, I need everyone get around her so we can lift her up and onto the blanket. Oh, and her body will probably be stiff, so don't let that freak you out," Howard said as he walked to the other side of Shanna's body.

"Don't let it freak us out?" Teek exclaimed. "It's a dead body!"

When the time came, they all joined in to move Shanna to

the blanket. Larry was at the head of the body. He looked into her clouded over eyes, open and seeming to stare right into his soul. He looked up and kept his attention on the others, jaws clenched as he helped carry her. When they set her down he moved away from the crowd and retched. The vomit was cloudy as if a lifetime of regret and pain left his body. Only sorrow remained.

Jemma looked at Shanna and then at her father's reaction. The scowl on her face spoke volumes.

"Okay, while Larry's recovering, why don't you four help me move her into my car?" Howard said.

They lifted the edges of the blanket and carried her to the car. Howard released his portion and opened the trunk.

"Just slide her in, uh, feet first is fine," Howard said as he noted the orientation of the body the kids were struggling to keep aloft. He ran around to the side and got in, folding down the rear bucket seat to make enough room for a stiff body. As the kids lifted her up, he crawled forward and grabbed the foot end of the blanket. He dragged it with the body as they tried to keep her lifted until she was all the way in.

Howard got out of the car and walked to the back to shut the trunk. All the kids were staring at Shanna.

"Is this how it's going to be with Granny Bael? We all lose our friends eventually until there's none left?" Jemma asked. She turned to look at her dad and the scowl returned.

"Don't be too hard on your dad," Howard said. "He and Shanna were an item before Granny put a stop to it. Well, before your grandfather locked him away for several years. We literally didn't see your dad for three years after. When we were all out of high school, we'd catch him every once in a while at the store. He usually avoided us, but he couldn't hide the bruises or the shame. His life was hell during that time, I have to imagine. On top of it all, he lost Shanna to Rick."

"So my mom was his second choice," Jemma said. "That explains a lot."

"Hey, I can't pretend to know what the relationship is between your parents, but I can't imagine he'd commit to marrying someone he didn't love. He was a great kid back then. Skeletons have a way of turning someone into something they're not," Howard said. He cleared his throat. "Let's get this cement poured, eh?" Howard said and shut the trunk gently. He glanced at Shanna briefly, her features fading with the light. The moment struck him then. Out of the six of them who had faced down Granny Bael all those years ago, three were dead. There were his friends and family, some closer than others, but all of them precious in his mind. Jemma's words echoed in his mind. Yes, that was how it was going to be until Granny Bael was no more.

He turned away and walked toward Larry, who had recovered mostly by now and was standing up straight again, looking up at the sky. Larry took out a handkerchief, wiped his eyes and then his mouth. He tossed the linen onto the ground and the wind caught it. It floated away into one of the broken structures.

"Larry, let's get going! It's getting dark. I'd like to be out of here before dark," Howard said.

"Yeah," Larry said. He turned and saw them walking toward him. "You kids go gather stuff to fill in these holes so the truck doesn't get stuck. Howard and I will get the forms set up."

"Can I help you instead, Dad?" Jemma asked. The other kids glanced at her in shock, but then turned away quickly.

"Sure," Larry said. "Be good for you to learn some vocational skills. Howard, why don't you help the kids gather stuff."

"Yeah, okay," Howard said as he looked at Jemma who just gave him a wan smile. "Probably better that way anyway."

Howard and the others went to search the wrecked buildings while Jemma joined her father at the cement truck.

There were boards secured behind the cab. Larry got them loose and then climbed into the cab to get tools. Jemma retrieved some boards and waited for her father to get back down.

"Dad, did Grandfather—" Jemma said.

"Your grandfather puts food on our table, don't you dare disrespect him. Choose your words carefully," Larry snapped. Jemma stared at him for a moment.

"So, you are a useless coward," Jemma said. She turned from him and carried the boards away.

Larry watched her back for a moment before retrieving a few boards to add to his load. He looked back at the patrol car and blinked. He stood for what seemed an eternity to him. He turned and followed Jemma.

The other kids returned with items from the buildings and put them in the holes. They brought broken, near rotted boards and chunks of cement from around the area, assembling a path for the truck to back over towards the sarcophagus.

Jemma dumped the new boards next to the sarcophagus away from the pool of blood. Larry approached and was about to say something but he noticed the blood and slowly walked around it. Jemma disappeared to grab the next load. Larry set everything down. He looked at the pool of blood again. He glanced at the patrol car. He clenched his teeth.

Coward.

The word swelled in his mind until he felt like his skull would burst. All his life, the same accusation came from every angle. Now it came from his own daughter. It grated on his already frayed nerves.

Mary broke off from the others and joined Jemma at the cement truck. They gathered the next load and walked toward the sarcophagus. Howard broke away from the boys as they finished packing the holes with debris. The adults and the girls converged in the middle.

"You're grounded after this," Larry said. "I told you to choose your words carefully."

"What happened?" Mary asked.

"I tried to ask him about Grandfather, but he cut me off, and then I called him a useless coward," Jemma said defiantly.

Mary turned to look at Larry and smirked. "She should have called you a useless ass wipe," Mary said and they continued on with their loads.

"Hey, there's no call for that language, young lady! I'm going to have a word with your parents!" Larry yelled. In response, Mary stopped and turned around. She raised both middle fingers while holding the boards she carried.

Larry looked at Howard.

"Kids these days have no respect for their elders," Larry said and shook his head.

"I don't think respect is automatic," Howard replied. "It's earned."

"Whatever," Larry snorted. "Let's get this shit show started. I've got a lot of paperwork to do when I get back."

Larry walked back to the cement truck as Howard turned to look at the girls. He looked back at Larry and started after him.

"Well, it's definitely a shit show," Howard murmured.

16
SECURED

The four kids built the forms at Larry's direction. The silence was trying for Larry even when it was punctuated by the occasional sarcastic scream from his daughter that they'd 'heard his directions.' The forms covered the lower eight feet of the sarcophagus. As they began wiring the steel rebar into place, Howard took a step back.

"Man, I shouldn't have brought you kids to this danger," Howard said. "I'm probably going to get fired for this."

"Uncle," Dom replied with a smile as he tightened wires. "You've just given us safe escort to a construction work site to learn valuable vocational skills."

"You remind me of Edward more and more every day, Dom. He was always an excellent bullshitter."

Dom and Teek laughed. The girls were less than enthusiastic.

"Girls, I know this is a lot," Howard started.

Mary stood up from her work.

"Officer Tulley, if—" Mary began, but Jemma put her hand up. She looked at her father and then at Howard.

"Officer, if we had irrefutable proof that my grandfather, Elbert Dawkins, was a murderer, would you even arrest him?"

"Jemma!" Larry shouted. She ignored him and watched Howard.

"I know who your grandfather is," Howard replied and chuckled nervously.

"You didn't answer the question," Jemma replied with a dead faced stare.

"Jemma, that's enough!" Larry yelled and walked toward his daughter.

"Answer the question!" She screamed with enough venom that it stopped Larry dead in his tracks. Howard looked at Larry and then back at Jemma. He looked down at the ground.

"Elbert Dawkins," Howard repeated the name though gritted teeth. He shook his head. "I mean, I'd have to see him kill someone with my own eyes and... then... shit. Case would be dumped into the circular file and never leave it. He's got his hooks into the city, surrounding counties and even the state police. My boss has said hands off Elbert Dawkins. He handles anything related to your grandfather."

"So, no?" Jemma sighed.

Larry frowned at Howard. Howard looked at Larry and shrugged his shoulders. "There have been dozens of complaints that disappeared. In some cases, the complainers disappeared as well. Devin Proctor went to the attorney general once, but they had to drop the case when Proctor and his family disappeared. I'm sorry. Elbert Dawkins is pretty much immune to prosecution."

"Never mind," Mary said abruptly. "One monster at a time." Jemma and Mary returned to their work.

Larry looked at them all with bewilderment. "This is bullshit," he murmured and walked away. "We're about done. Time to pour the cement and end this."

Howard watched Larry walk away and sighed. He set his hand down briefly on his side arm in the holster and then shook his head. He'd made an oath to serve and protect the citizens of Tuggville, but it seemed like the only one who got protected was Elbert Dawkins. He'd given them a false number of the cases pushed under the rug in regards to Elbert Dawkins. Murder, extortion, rape, assault, abuse, false imprisonment—the charges were in the hundreds, not just the dozens and they went back decades since well before Howard was a cop.

He turned back to the kids who stepped back from their work. The sarcophagus was now surrounded by a six foot high wall of plywood and two by fours with steel rebar poking up out of the top.

"I think we got this, but if it goes south, run as fast as you can to Abigail. She'll know what to do," Howard said.

"Crazy Abby?" Teek asked. "The psychic on the other side of town?"

"Hey," Mary said as she punched Teek in the arm. "That's my aunt."

"So, she's not crazy?" Teek asked.

"No, she's crazy, but only my family can call her crazy."

"Okay, that's enough," Howard said. "She's had it rough in life. Dealing with this madness would make anyone unhinged. Can't say any of us were ever in our right mind again after that night. I don't know how you could be. But if anyone has a handle on capturing Granny Bael again, it's Abigail. So promise me you'll do it. Go see her."

"We'll go see her, Uncle," Dom said. "Does she live in a gingerbread house?"

"Just like your Uncle Ed," Howard groaned. "Be nice to her when you see her. For me, okay?"

"Sure thing, Uncle," Dom said and gave him a genuine smile.

The cement truck got closer as it backed up over the debris filled holes. Howard turned to direct Larry back and gave him thumbs up when he'd gotten close enough to the forms. Larry jumped out and maneuvered the discharge chute into place, advising the kids what controls to work on the truck.

"I'm going to take Shanna back now," Howard said as the cement began to pour into the forms. Larry shook his hand solemnly.

"I can take the kids back in the truck," Larry told him. "Plenty of room in the cab."

"Cool," Howard said. "I'll be glad when this day is over."

"You and me both," Larry replied.

Howard walked to the patrol car. He took one last look as the cement truck finished pumping and Larry walked around to inspect the forms. Howard climbed in his vehicle and took off.

Howard watched the sarcophagus fade in the rearview mirror as he pulled away. He took a deep breath as he focused on the growing fog illuminated by the headlights on the darkened roadway. The whisper of the tires on the wet pavement calmed him.

"Elbert Dawkins," Howard said as he reached for the radio to call in. "You're no saint, but are you a killer?"

17

CREMATION

"Everything looks sturdy," Jemma announced as her father came back from his inspection on the other side of the forms.

Larry nodded. "It will do until we can get the crew out here in a couple days," Larry said as he walked to the cement truck. He motioned for the kids to get in.

"What are you going to tell them?" Jemma asked.

"Nothing much," Larry responded as he opened the door for them to all climb in from his side. "I'll just give them the specs to build a larger, thicker dome around this. Something quake proof. Tell them there are hazardous chemicals inside."

"Well, that's no lie," Jemma said and laughed just a little as she climbed in, the last of the kids.

Larry chuckled as he climbed up into the cab. He shut the door and looked at Jemma. She sat there with a grim but hopeful look. He smiled as he thought back to the days of rocking her to sleep as a baby, cuddling her along with Diedre on cold nights in front of the fireplace. Days long gone and never to return.

"Jemma, I'm sorry I haven't been the best father."

"Doesn't seem like there are many of those in Tuggville." Jemma sighed.

"Your grandfather, I know he's not a good man, but he's very powerful."

"Here," Jemma replied forcefully. "He's powerful here."

"Well, yeah, but we can't just leave. Everything we know is here."

"We can just leave. You, Mom, me, Emily, and Derek. We can just up and leave tomorrow."

"It's not that simple," Larry said. "You're maybe too young to understand."

"Grandfather threatened our families if Mary and I won't have sex with him Saturday," Jemma blurted out. Tears started flowing and she covered her mouth, choking down a sob.

"What the fuck?" Dom said. Teek just sat there with his mouth open. He looked at Mary, who sat next to him on the passenger side of the cab. She looked out the window and wouldn't meet his gaze.

"Mary, is this true?" Larry asked. He stared straight ahead. He didn't want to believe it, but in his heart, he knew it was more likely true than not. His mind traveled back to sitting in the safe room. The monitor showed Abigail being dragged through the hallway leading away from the ballroom by the two security guards who hounded his every step before it cycled away to a different camera view. He didn't see her again or hear anything from his soundproof room.

"Elbert Dawkins," Mary said, staring out the window, "is a pedophile rapist son of a bitch."

"Oh shit," Teek said. "That's fucked up."

Dom touched Jemma's hand. "Is that what you were asking my uncle about?" Dom asked.

Mary turned to look at them. "And your uncle basically said he'd get away with it," she said with a tremor in her voice.

A flicker of movement in the rearview mirror caught Howard's attention. He put the radio back in the holder and gave the rearview mirror his full attention. Shanna's dead eyes looked back at him and then began to glow red.

"Elbert and his accomplices will burn for their sins!" Shanna mouthed the words, but the screeching voice was Granny Bael's. Her head erupted in flame with a hideous scream.

The patrol car exploded in a ball of fire and slowly came to rest on the side of the road, the inferno growing to a white hot flame. It lit up the night sky like it was day.

The explosion a mile down the road from the District caught everyone's attention in the cab of the cement truck.

"Uncle Howard!" Dom shouted.

Larry started up the truck and threw it into gear, making a horrendous grinding sound as he slammed on the accelerator forcing the protesting vehicle into a quick start. They tore through part of the broken fence as they came around the corner. Even as they did, they could see the column of flame and smoke rising just ahead on the road.

"Shit," Larry said as he accelerated at a slower pace. "Okay, Jemma, listen to me. You need to take care of Mom and your brother and sister."

"What?" Jemma asked.

"I'm going to stop your grandfather for good. He's hurt too many people," Larry said and then looked at them. "All of you promise me you'll help each other through this. It's not gonna be pretty."

"So, just an average day in Tuggville, then," Teek smirked.

"Teek!" Mary yelled.

"All right!" Teek shouted. "Our lives are all kinds of shitty, right? We gotta stick together anyway just to get through it."

"Yeah," Larry replied. "That about covers it."

The truck rolled up to the remaining bits and shell of Howard's patrol car. The gas tank had ruptured, blowing much of the vehicle to pieces. The trunk door still smoldered where it sat ten feet behind the car.

Larry steered around the burning debris and stopped the truck. He opened the door and stepped down from the truck. Jemma and Dom came after. Dom ran toward the inferno, but the extreme heat stopped him from getting too close.

"Uncle Howard!" Dom shouted at the flames. Barely discernible in the driver's seat was what appeared to be a burning figure, though it was nearly skeletal at this point.

Dom fell to his knees as the memories of the fishing and camping trips with his uncle came back to him. The uncle who became a surrogate father to him because his own dad couldn't handle the pressures of what Tuggville had done to him. He was the one person who rescued him from tortuous hours withstanding the verbal assaults and accusations of his step father. His only real role model in a town filled with hate and despair. The tears came flooding down his cheeks as the future he'd have with his uncle evaporated in an instant.

The other kids gathered around him and hugged him as he struggled to stay up. All his energy seemed to be funneled into his screaming sorrow.

After a few minutes, Teek patted Dom on the back and said, "I think this qualifies as things going south."

"What does that mean?" Larry asked.

"We have to go see crazy Abby—she can stop this," Dom said.

"Abigail? The psychic? She was a nice lady. She and Howard were an item until…" Larry said.

"What happened?" Jemma asked.

"Elbert Dawkins happened," Mary said.

Larry went pale. He nodded slowly. "I was locked in my room. I saw her dragged away against her will. I didn't see or hear anything else, but after that day, she stopped talking to anyone in town. Started up a phone psychic business and only took out of town calls."

Larry fell back against the truck. "Diedre, my God…" he whispered.

"Dad?" Jemma asked. She got up from Dom's side and ran to her father.

"She started having memory issues just a few weeks after

we were married. We'd been staying at father's estate until the house he arranged for us was ready. I was always away at work... but he wasn't always at the office. Said he had business to attend to. She became pregnant and we thought that was the cause of the memory problems, but then after you were born, she went to see a therapist. But nothing changed until your brother and sister came along. She stopped going to the therapist and began drinking. She said her memory came back and I was a coward. I let him do that to her. She didn't talk to me for weeks. But she never said who or what..."

"Dad, I don't understand," Jemma said.

"That son of a bitch." Larry got up, his face turning red. "You kids go to Abby—tell her to get that fucking Granny bottled back up. I'm going to take care of Grandpa," he said the last word like he was spitting up a slug. He hugged Jemma and then jumped into the truck.

"Wait! What—" Jemma hollered but Larry started the truck up and slammed his foot on the accelerator. Jemma jumped back from the truck. Larry didn't even look at her. His focus was completely on his own vengeance now.

"Well," Mary said, getting up and tugging on Dom's arm. "Let's go."

"I think we should've asked for a ride," Teek said. "Crazy Abby is on the other side of town."

"Shit," Dom said as he stood up, wiping his face. He took one last look at the burning car and then started walking away toward town. "We gotta lock this Granny bitch down."

18

LINE IN THE SALT

Larry pulled into the cement plant and parked the truck where it normally sat waiting to be loaded. He took the keys, hung them up on the board in the production room and then headed for the corporate office building. It sat separate from the actual cement production facilities to reduce the vibration from the production machines. The entire corporate office building had been lined with soundproofing tiles and thick, soundproof windows to reduce the noise from the factory. Stepping into those offices was like visiting another realm. It was cool and quiet in the summer, warm and inviting in the winter. Today, it felt more like entering a mummy's tomb—cold, dark and foreboding.

Larry walked up the two flights of stairs to the executive suite on the third floor. The whole floor was dedicated solely to the President of the company, Elbert Hawkins. Shiny trophies and plaques lined the walls, all accomplishments that rang hollow considering Elbert's connections, influence, and power. It was all part of the window dressing for a man who demanded respect and severely punished those who didn't offer it without complaint.

The hallway lined with accolades all funneled to a set of large oak doors emblazoned with a gold plaque that read *Elbert Dawkins, President.* Larry didn't even knock—the absolute minimum required protocol when entering Elbert's office. He hoped it would set the old man on edge, catch him off balance. Instead, what he saw when he opened the door stopped Larry cold.

Elbert raised a shotgun to Larry entering the room. When the old man noticed it was Larry, he lowered it and chuckled. "I thought it was someone important coming to pay their respects," Elbert said. "Instead, it's my pathetic, ungrateful son. What miserable tidings do you bring on the heels of your protocol ignorance?"

Larry took in the room. The large oak desk was surrounded by a thick circle of what Larry assumed was salt. He took it the old man had been expecting Granny Bael. "I came to warn you," Larry said. "That your time had come."

"I assume you failed to secure Granny Balsom in her heretical form; I'm not really surprised. You continue to fail me on a regular basis," Elbert said. "I'll deal with the fire witch when she arrives. It won't be the first time." Elbert looked at Larry's clenched fists and raised his eyebrows. "Oh, I see you've suddenly found some backbone! Your little bitch daughter told you about our agreement?"

"You're a sick, twisted bastard!" Larry screamed.

Elbert howled with a laughter that was pure in its mirth and enjoyment all while raising the shotgun at Larry. In his rage, Larry ignored the gun and took a step forward. Elbert clicked the gun's safety off and the sound refocused Larry's attention on the weapon. He stopped his forward momentum.

"You really don't have a horse in this race, my son. You see, Jemma isn't even a blood relation to you," Elbert said. "She is a full blooded Dawkins, though."

"So I'd guessed," Larry said with a scowl. "Rape, murder, incest—is there anything you won't sink to to get your perverted rocks off?"

"No," Elbert replied. "Of course, those that truly understand the full extent of who and what I am rarely live to do anything about it."

Elbert fired the shotgun into Larry's chest, knocking him off his feet and onto the ground.

"Well," Elbert said. "I needed to replace this carpet anyway."

Mary led the way up the street to the cottage that sat alone at the end of the lonely road. Trees lined the road and surrounded the small building. As they approached, they saw concentric circles of white around the building. Small half tube enclosures of clear plastic or glass protected the particles inside from the elements, maintaining a secure set of protections against entities both seen and unseen.

The cottage itself was white and brown, wood frame construction, and perhaps twelve hundred square feet altogether—more if there was a basement but none could be seen externally. The front porch was lined with wind chimes and different fetishes, while the windows were adorned with multiple symbols and dream catchers. It seemed like every type of mystical protection that could be conceived had been deployed.

Mary walked up the central walk and knocked on the door. Teek followed while Jemma and Dom brought up the rear. Jemma, however, stopped at the outer circle abruptly as if blocked by an invisible barrier.

"What the hell?" Jemma said and Dom turned around to see Jemma standing just outside the outer white circle with one hand on her stomach. She backed a few steps away from the outer circle. Mary seemed unaware of Jemma's issue and knocked loudly on the door.

"Aunt Abigail? We need your help!" Mary shouted as she continued pounding on the door.

The door swung open and a pale blonde woman wearing a white billowy top and a dark patterned skirt peered with disdain through round glasses at Mary. "What do you want? I'm busy. Go away and make an appointment," Abigail said gruffly and moved to close the door. Mary shoved her foot in the open space to stop the door.

"Aunt Abigail, it's me, Mary," the girl said, much quieter than the shouting she'd done earlier.

Abigail squinted at Mary and examined her face. Her scowl lost some of its menace and she relaxed. "Oh, well I'm still busy. Don't people call anymore?"

"Granny Bael is loose," Mary said.

"I know," Abigail replied with a smile. "What do you think I'm busy with?"

"You're going to help us trap her?" Mary asked.

"Not just yet, she hasn't done what I require of her," Abigail said and then looked at Jemma; her eyes got wide. She rushed past Mary and Teek and approached Jemma cautiously. She stopped next to Dom just inside the outer circle and gave him a brief glance before returning her attention to Jemma.

Jemma looked warily at the older woman. She noted the worry lines deeply entrenched on the psychic's face. Abigail appeared older than her forty-two years of age.

"What are you?" Abigail asked and scratched her head. She looked Jemma up and down, but got no closer to her, taking great care to stay within the outer circle. Abigail cocked her head. Jemma felt her head begin to tingle.

"Doesn't matter," Abigail said abruptly and waved her hands. "You're not welcome here, whatever you are. I've got pressing matters to attend to. Now leave."

Abigail turned and went back toward her house.

"You have to help us," Mary said.

"She killed my Uncle Howard," Dom said.

Abigail stopped abruptly. She raised a hand to her mouth and it quivered. She turned to look at Dom with tears in her eyes. "I should've known. The family resemblance is unmistakable. Poor Howard," she said and then turned back to walk slowly to the house. "We all pay the price for our foolishness eventually."

"We have to stop her!" Mary cried.

"No!" Abigail said as she stepped up to Mary. "Not until she has destroyed him."

"Destroyed who?" Mary asked.

"Elbert Dawkins. He's next. Once he's finished, then we can begin the process," she grabbed Mary's arm and reached into her pocket. She fished out a set of keys and handed them to Mary. She looked at Jemma and frowned. She reached back into her pocket, pulled out a necklace and handed it to Mary as well. "Take my car—go out to the family ranch. All has been prepared. Your mother is there now. And you—" she pointed at Jemma. "Wear this necklace or you'll never get into the ranch. I think you'll be okay with the car, though."

"But what about you?" Mary asked.

"She'll come for me after Elbert if everyone else is gone already. Academically, I wonder if she'll attempt to find Troy after we're gone. Anyway, if I don't entrap her spirit, you'll be the last line of defense. She'll come after you all next," Abigail stopped and looked at Teek. She looked at Jemma and back at Teek. "Why does she have it and you don't? Curious."

Teek looked dumbfounded. He watched in silence as Abigail retreated back inside and shut the door.

"Have what?" Teek asked. Mary shook her head. She grabbed Teek's hand and pulled him toward Dom.

"Let's get to the ranch," Mary said. "I don't like this one bit."

They all climbed into the beige four door sedan with strange symbols drawn all over it. The inside smelled like burned candles and incense.

"Ah," Teek said. "Smells like success."

Everyone groaned as Mary started the car.

19
CLOSURE

Abigail set her back against the front door and wept. She allowed herself only a minute or two to acknowledge her grief. Howard had meant the world to her but after Elbert's violation she just couldn't allow anyone else to touch her, couldn't allow anyone else to whisper in her ear about how attractive she was, how good her body felt beneath theirs. She simply didn't have the capacity to get beyond it.

She sniffed, wiped her eyes and walked through her living room filled with charms and crystals. She was certain the mystical energies were the only thing that kept her sane. That and the protections around the house that kept evil at bay. Elbert Dawkins couldn't get by the protections anymore than Granny Bael could. His evil predator aura was bold and obvious, making it easy to block with the proper incantations and wards.

She considered the Dawkins child. She'd seen her aura and the evil wasn't obvious. It was something deep inside. She could feel the menace, but it wasn't directed at her. It was well hidden. She shook her head.

"One monster at a time, Abigail," she whispered as she entered the kitchen and set her eye to the eyepiece of the telescope pointed at Elbert Dawkins' office atop the cement company building. "Where are you, sweet Granny Bael?"

Elbert looked at Larry prone on the floor. The blood pooling on his chest soaked through his shirt, but Elbert could see he was still breathing. He considered using a second shot, but he needed it for his next visitor. There was only so much salted buckshot handy. He loaded another cartridge into the empty chamber and closed the shotgun again. Two shots would give her pause.

Elbert sighed as he looked at the open door. "Couldn't even shut the door behind you? Honestly, what kind of manners did you retain in that thick skull of yours anyway," Elbert said to the unconscious Larry.

An orange glow began to grow down the hallway. It grew in intensity and filled the doorway until the burning face of Granny Bael appeared. The flames outlined a body dressed in red robes that flowed in the air like gossamer wisps of ash. Fire shimmered on the surface of a dark dress beneath the robes that wasn't consumed but seemed to ebb and flow with the heat of the flames. Her attention wavered briefly to the body on the floor. She gave Elbert a dark smile and raised her hand.

"Wasn't enough to kill my family, but now you murder your own? Pathetic," she said.

"Hardly my family, certainly not blood, and he repaid my generosity for pulling him from an orphanage and getting every advantage in life by being a failure. Good riddance," Elbert replied. He raised the shotgun and pointed it at her. "My father failed as well because you're clearly still kicking."

"So you don't know?" Granny cackled. "How interesting. The secrets your family keeps."

"Don't know what?" Elbert replied. "You know what, I don't even care." Elbert fired first one shot and then the second at Granny sending her screaming backward into the hallway.

She shook it off in seconds and returned to the door way. "Failure must be a family trait," Granny cackled as she glowed brighter.

"I enjoyed ruining your granddaughters before I killed them," Elbert sneered. "They cried out for their Granny to protect them."

Granny screeched and fire erupted from her hands, but an invisible shield blocked it from reaching Elbert. She looked down at the line of salt.

"Such a simple compound for keeping the unworthy at bay," Elbert said as he laughed. "Your grandchildren would weep at your pitiful attempt at vengeance. You should look elsewhere for satisfaction."

Granny looked at down at Larry, who had regained consciousness and crawled toward the salt circle. She looked back up at Elbert and smiled. "My grandchildren will know vengeance this night, Elbert Dawkins."

Elbert glanced down at Larry. The old man's eyebrows

shot up as his son drug a bloody hand through the salt, breaking the circle.

"No!" Elbert shouted.

Larry looked up at his father and smiled grimly.

"The unworthy win the day," he said and his head slumped to the ground.

Granny screeched and a jet of flame billowed out from her body, engulfing the entire room. Elbert screamed as his clothing burned away and ebony bubbles of his flesh burst like pimples. Within several agony-drenched minutes, Elbert's screams were finally cut off as his blackened and desiccated corpse fell to the ground.

Larry was mercifully dead before the inferno cremated his body and the entire upper floor of the building. It collapsed within a few moments onto the second floor, which then brought the whole building down. Granny Bael glowed brightly, turning night into day once again, before drifting slowly to the ground seeking her next target.

Abigail watched the top of the office building explode and collapse. She observed Granny floating down from the inferno and disappearing from sight.

"Way to go, old fire witch," Abigail said. "I think you'll find I won't fall quite so easily." Abigail rushed around her cottage, closing shutters and setting charms just so on the shelves on each wall. She lit candles and sat down in the center of the building with a bowl of water in front of her. She struck a pose of deep meditation and slowed her breathing.

She flushed her mind of thoughts of Howard and their

love lost decades ago. The memory of his tender hand upon her cheek, their first kiss by the apple orchard and his profession of love before the school dance all washed away. Her sorrow at his passing and pride at the bravery he must've exhibited in those final moments she had to push from her mind. All emotions she felt for Howard Tulley had to pass away for her mind to focus.

The harder memories, the ones with the most anger and betrayal attached to them, were devoted to Elbert Dawkins. With his passing, though, she found it easier to eliminate the impressions of torture and rape she suffered at his hands. His vile breath upon her neck, his vulgar smell invading her nostrils, and the nauseating sound of his exultant voice at her defeat and submission to his desires were discarded with no little effort from her psyche. She breathed through the elation she felt at his demise and let it pass as well, reaching a place of calm and serenity. She concentrated on the surface of the water and it revealed the burning form of Granny Bael as she passed through the town.

In the old witch's mind, Abigail's soothing voice interrupted Granny's vile thoughts of vengeance upon her. "Granny Balsom, thank you for your service in eliminating the thrice damned Elbert Dawkins. You may rest in peace now. Your vengeance has been fulfilled."

Granny Bael stopped and looked around. She returned her focus on finding Abigail's cottage and moved forward. "You think my vengeance is spent? Your families denied me vengeance for decades! This town sheltered my family's killer while they falsely accused me and burned me at the stake! My thirst for vengeance is nowhere near quenched and I'll start with you, Abigail!" she screamed into the night.

"I respect your power and your pain," Abigail's soothing voice continued. "But there has been enough death and destruction wrought upon this town. I beseech you reconsider, lest you be trapped again or have your soul torn asunder and flung to the four winds."

"You don't have that kind of power, witch!" Granny cried out in frustration.

"I have foreseen it, Granny. Find your peace now or you may never see it."

"Deceit!" Granny screeched. "You'll burn for your lies, witch!"

"Isn't that what they shouted at you so many years ago?"

"Enough!" Granny screamed and a jet of flame burst through the surface of the water in the scrying bowl, narrowly missing Abigail's head as she fell to the side. The curtains behind her lit up.

"Shit!" Abigail growled. She jumped up and tossed the water from the bowl onto the curtains, putting out the small fire. "No more Ms. Nice Witch," Abigail whispered. She grabbed a small copper bowl and a bag of items from a shelf to her right and sat back down in the center of the room.

Granny Bael got to the outer ring of salt surrounding Abigail's abode and hissed. She tested the defenses of the cottage and found them firmly entrenched.

Abigail dropped items into the copper bowl speaking words of enchantment. The items in the bowl began to ignite.

Granny Bael felt her substance begin to unravel; her anger

failed to be enough to hold her solely in this realm. She began to cross over.

"No! I'm not done yet!" Granny screamed.

Inside the house, Abigail smiled. "Oh yes you are..."Abigail smirked as she reached into the bag for the last few ingredients.

Granny looked around at the grove of trees adjacent to the humble residence and cackled.

"Do you think I need to kill you directly with fire when you've provided me with so many other ways to destroy you, clever little witch?!" Granny screeched. She threw open her arms and a ring of fire burst out from her, surrounding the house and lighting all the nearby trees on fire.

Abigail's chants rouse in volume as she rushed to finish the ritual.

With another burst of energy from Granny, the tree trunks all cracked and fell in on Abigail's house, destroying it and burying the psychic under mounds of rubble. Powers lines fell, sparking more fires and cutting out lights across the town. Granny pushed forward but was still rebuffed by the circle of salt protecting the building. She growled. "So be it, witch. Suffer the enduring agony of having the air crushed from your trapped body as I did in that insufferable barrel!" Granny screamed and sent a torrent of flame up into the night air, lighting it up for all to see from miles away.

Mary saw the column of flame rise into the night sky behind them in the mirror as she pressed on the accelerator. The others turned as they felt the sonic wave accompanying the explosion of flame ripple through the town.

"That'll be the last of them," Mary said as the words caught in her throat. She swallowed hard. Her aunt had almost always been distant, but she was always kind when Mary had visited her at the cottage as rare as that might've been. Knowing Aunt Abby was her last refuge when her mother passed hurt more as her relative burned away in the night. The tears at her loss and the pain of things to come flooded down her cheeks. She wiped a hand across her cheekbones.

"It's up to us now," she whispered.

"We're strong," Jemma said and grabbed her hand.

"We're fucked," Teek said as he turned away from the fading column of fire. "Why don't we just keep driving out of town, away from it all?"

"Dude," Dom said. "Crazy Abby made a contingency plan. She must've known what would happen. She slowed Granny Bael down for us. We have to go on in her memory—in all of their memories."

"We've all lost loved ones tonight," Mary said as she turned onto the dirt road leading to the ranch. "Let's make sure their sacrifices weren't in vain."

"She'd find us wherever we go," Jemma whispered and sat back in her seat looking out the window at the dark night, wishing it would swallow her up and take her away from everything.

20
RANCH HANDS

As the car entered the ranch, the kids noticed the fence and various rocks littered around bore some of the same symbols drawn on the car.

"This isn't what it looked like last time I was here," Mary said.

"When was that?" Jemma asked.

"Before high school," Mary said. "Before the divorce."

"Ow! Stop the car!" Jemma cried out and pushed herself back in the seat. Mary stopped the car. Jemma pushed open the door and climbed out of the car. She walked a few steps back toward the main road and held her stomach.

The others got out of the car. Dom ran to her side.

"What is it?" He asked.

"Pain," Jemma said, gasping as she held her abdomen. "It happened as soon as we got near the fence. It was like that at Abby's but this is worse."

"Oh," Mary said. She pulled the necklace out of her

pocket and handed it to Jemma. "That must be why you're supposed to wear the necklace."

"Why don't any of you have to wear one?" Jemma asked as she held the necklace in her hand like a dead fish.

"Well, she had a problem with your grandfather, maybe the ranch is protected against members of the Dawkins family?" Dom said.

"Put it on," Mary said. "Let's see if it helps."

"Why not?" Jemma asked. She slid the necklace over her head and gasped. A surreal feeling flowed down her body like water. She'd never felt so at peace. "Wow," she said as she walked forward and passed the car with no discomfort. "I think your aunt could make a killing selling these necklaces!"

"Okay, we'll suggest it after we fight off the demon witch and resurrect my aunt," Mary replied. "Come on. Get back in the car and we'll go slowly, just in case."

They all got back in the car and Jemma relaxed in the car seat. She sighed as she absently caressed the necklace. "Think this thing has weed in it?" Jemma asked.

"If it doesn't smell like ass, probably not," Teek replied.

"Dude," Dom said.

Mary laughed and started the car forward. After she edged forward a few feet with Jemma feeling no ill effects, Mary slowly accelerated to a normal speed and they continued down the dirt road.

Mary pulled the sedan to a stop and looked at the porch of the old ranch house. The faded red color of the building was hard to make out in the dark, but the headlights illuminated the peeling condition of the paint well. The ranch house wasn't well taken care of. Mary didn't remember the last time they'd been there. Uncle Wayne was a bit of a loner.

The rickety wooden door with half the screen torn up opened slowly. Uncle Wayne with a full head of hair turned white, wearing coveralls, a red flannel shirt and cowboy boots, stepped out and held the door open for Mary's mother, who struggled to step outside. She was pale, thin and struggled with the effort of moving. Her paper thin flower dress seemed to whip around in the mild wind of the evening. Mary's breath caught in her throat.

"Shit," Mary whispered. She turned off the car and got out quickly. She ran to the porch and hugged her mom. The other kids got out of the car and stood by watching. Bits of their own families had been torn away from them today, but Mary had to watch the slow deterioration of her mother over months.

Uncle Wayne waved at them from the porch and they walked forward like they had lead shoes. The adrenaline rush from the last hour was wearing off and they could feel the weight of the day pressing down on all of them.

Mary hurried her mom inside to sit down on a chair. She kneeled at her feet and rested her head in her mom's lap. Her mother whispered softly to her and stroked her hair gently.

"You kids can rest in the guest rooms. It's a big house. Bigger than I need," Wayne said and pointed down the hallway. The inside of the house was well kept, simple and utilitarian, furnished in the trappings of the 1950s. Chairs had been reupholstered, but never replaced. The wallpaper had seen better days and was worn at the edges, but seemed well maintained otherwise.

The kids shuffled over the green carpet down the hallway. Jemma pulled Dom into a bedroom with her and she quietly shut the door. Teek didn't even seem to notice as he wandered off like a zombie into a room further down the hall.

"Jemma, we shouldn't—" Dom began to say.

Jemma put her fingers to his lips to stop his protest. "We don't even know if we'll live through tomorrow," Jemma said fiercely, her eyes glistening with tears.

Dom took her face in his hands and kissed her gently. "Okay, if you're sure," he said. "You make a compelling argument," he added with a grin. "Were you in debate club?"

Jemma giggled as she turned off the light.

Teek stripped off his wet and dirty clothes and collapsed on the bed. He was asleep almost as soon as his head hit the pillow.

His sleep was anything but restful.

In the hazy fog of his subconscious, the faces of his foster siblings came into focus. Off in the distance, he heard the angry screams of his foster parents. The accusations flew readily at them all. Vile cursing at the kids, even the youngest, was common in their household as they were warned to behave or face the punishment of the basement.

Teek glanced in their direction and noticed they screamed from behind bars. Their anger still present but muted by the overdue interception of law enforcement. Given it was Tuggville, even Teek thought it wouldn't last and they'd be back at their greedy, child abusing ways before long.

He turned back to his siblings and noticed some of them had Xs made of black tape across their eyes. They all tugged on his hands and clothes, bringing him closer to the back building which had been miraculously restored to its intact though dilapidated state.

As they entered the building, the familiar scent of the grimy carpet assaulted his nose. The walls had stains on them from things he could never place. The windows were taped together where the glass had broken. Some of the windows had been boarded up entirely. It was nothing he hadn't seen before. It was all too hauntingly familiar. He mused he wouldn't miss it now that it had been destroyed.

He looked at the kids with the black Xs over their eyes. The cost of the destruction was maybe too much.

The kids pulled him to the lone inner door in the kitchen, the triple dead-bolted inner door that led to the basement. It was slightly ajar and a sickly green light emanated from below. The kids pushed him to the threshold, then stopped and waited. He looked down the stairs to a glowing green fog roiling along the floor. He shook his head.

He turned his back on the doorway and faced the children now gathered in a semi-circle around him. They all pointed at the doorway and open their mouths to speak, but blood simply poured from within them, dripping down their clothes, sticking to the hand me down garments like crimson syrup. Teek turned away from them quickly.

He stepped onto the stairs and heard the familiar creak of the old wood under his feet. He'd been down here once before, locked in one of the hell boxes for three days with no food and only a bowl full of water. There had been a bucket placed in a hole in the ground to relieve himself in. Otherwise, he just sat or lay on the dirt floor waiting for day to come when a few stray rays of sunlight pierced the gaps in the wooden walls.

He never complained about not getting enough food to eat ever again and kept the younger children from making the same mistake.

The green fog led to a single hell box far across the basement. The box was in a dark corner that Teek was pretty sure never got any sunlight. He was marginally thankful he hadn't been put in that one. As he walked along the path, things crunched beneath his feet. It sounded like the path was lined with crackers and pretzels, but they were hidden beneath the strange green cloud.

Teek reached the box and stood there staring at it. The padlock on the latch was open but still in place. It wouldn't take much effort to remove it and open the door, but Teek couldn't seem to bring his arms up to remove the lock.

The lock slowly rose up out of the latch hole on its own and dropped to the ground when it came free. The latch fell open and the door slowly swung toward Teek as it opened. Daniel, his missing foster brother, lay there; his starved body stacked on a pile of bones. The bones shifted and Daniel's body rolled toward Teek, the empty eye sockets in the skull looking up at him as worms crawled out of them.

Teek screamed.

Wayne touched Mary's shoulder and she raised her head. Her mother's hand slid limply off Mary's head into her mother's lap. Mary choked and raised her hand to her mouth.

"It's okay. She's just sleeping," Wayne said.

Mary looked at her mother's chest and saw it rise slowly and briefly as her mother took shallow breaths in her sleep.

Wayne lifted Mary's elbow and she stood up. "You need to rest too," he said gently. "There's a battle ahead and you'll need your strength."

Mary looked at her uncle and noticed his gaunt features for the first time. "Uncle Wayne!" She gasped as she touched the thin skin on his face.

"Fracking chemicals polluted the ground water. The well," he gestured toward the back of the ranch house. "I haven't got much time left either, but I'm pretty sure your mother will pass first. I had enough strength to help Abigail put up the protections around the ranch, but they'll only last so long. They weren't designed to protect us forever." He touched her head gently and kissed her forehead. "Now go get some rest," Wayne said. "Tomorrow will be your time to shine, little one."

Mary nodded and hugged him. She let him go and looked at her mother again. She looked comfortable and at peace. If she passed in the night, but no—Mary wasn't ready to think about that just yet. She rushed down the hall and heard Teek moaning in a bedroom to the right. She looked in and saw him tossing about in the bed.

She smiled as she entered the room. She closed the door and removed her own clothes and lay next to him. As her skin touched his, he calmed down and seemed to return to a more restful sleep. She cuddled up next to him and fell into her own slumber.

21
SEARCHING

Granny Bael walked into the town square and looked around. The damaged structures were being attended to by shop owners and workmen even at this late hour. But the lights were out, power cut to the entire town by the earthquake damage to the frail infrastructure; people worked by flashlight and lantern. As Granny's glow became apparent, eyes swiveled to observe the fiery witch walking by the fountain in the center of the square. As soon as they saw her, they started running away.

Granny closed her eyes and concentrated, but she couldn't sense the four she sought. "Where *are* they?!" she screamed as she opened her eyes. Rivers of fire flowed down the streets and encircled the entire town square, capturing buildings, vehicles and the people trying to escape on foot. The ones on foot sought shelter within the broken buildings, hiding from Granny the best they could.

She walked to the nearest car. The man inside ducked

down when she approached. Granny placed her hand on the driver's side window and it melted into a pool of slag at her touch. The man inside scrambled to the passenger side door. As he tried to open it, Granny huffed and a cloud of smoke burst forth from her mouth falling over him like a blanket. The man froze in place and looked back at her.

"Where are the children—Dawkins, Tulley and Verdoon?" Granny screeched.

"I don't know what you're talking about!" the man screamed back. His hands fumbled at the door handle in a full out panic.

"Then you're of no use to me," Granny Bael said and the interior of the car erupted in fire.

The man's screams lasted less than a minute as the fire consumed him. Granny smiled at the sounds until he finally went silent. "I'll burn you all until I find the information I want!" she screamed into the night air. Shouts of panic echoed through the broken alleys and streets as people burrowed into their hiding places and then went silent.

"I know where you all are," Granny announced. "That bitch Crazy Abby didn't protect you from my wrath. Why would you protect those stupid fucking kids?!"

"We don't know what you're talking about, demon from hell!" a man shouted from his hiding place.

"Then you burn!" Granny shouted and the building the man was hiding in suddenly exploded as Granny's jet of flame in his direction lit a pocket of gas from a broken pipe. As the debris fell from the sky and hit the pavement, Granny laughed.

"Wilson, McGillicutty, Franklin—all of your families

participated in my birth fifty years ago when you burned *me* at the stake! Do you think you deserve anything less than to die by fire?" Granny screamed. As the surnames of some of the people were said, they all flinched and their eyes went wide.

"But I can make your death quick or slow, depending on whether I find out where those accursed children are!"

Slowly, methodically, and with pinpoint accuracy, Granny found each person hiding within the ring of fire surrounding Tuggville's town center. As the burned corpses accumulated, their blackened flesh smoked, adding a torturous smell to the air. Some people lost their minds entirely and ran for the edges of the town square, dying as they were consumed by the wall of flames that met them there.

As each body piled up, Granny's rage grew. It took time to pull out each person and torture them to death. She'd gained no information from the pathetic townsfolk pleading for mercy she had no intention of providing. Hours passed and she was no closer to her quarry. Sunrise approached; she could feel it tugging at her mind. The light would flood the landscape and her powers would wane.

"Where are they?!" she screamed at her next victim, an elderly man who held up a walker trying to defend himself.

"I don't know! Please, don't hurt me!" the old man cried out.

"Why do you all defy me?!" Granny screamed as she vented a stream of fire at the old man so hot his blood boiled in seconds. His flesh exploded across the walls and onto another person cowering in a corner of the alley they were in. The burning bits pelted the hapless observer and they howled in pain as the lava hot shrapnel hit their flesh and set fire to their clothing.

Wayne woke up as the phone rang. He struggled to stand up from his chair as his sister tossed fitfully in her chair. He walked over to the phone hanging on the wall and picked it up. "Hello?"

"It's Murphy," came the voice on the other end of the phone. "I'm surprised this line is working."

"Where are you?"

Murphy glanced out the window of the library. Across the street, there was a thick wall of fire. "I watched her from the second story of the library. Dozens of people slaughtered, one at a time. I don't know what she's doing, but I hope you've got a plan," Murphy said. He wiped his face, drying the fresh tears from his face.

Wayne looked at the clock on the wall. It read 6:15 A.M. He nodded.

"We'll get this stopped. I'll drop the wards and she'll come here. God help us we can end this once and for all," Wayne replied. He hung up the phone, walked to his sister and pressed his hand on her shoulder until she woke.

"It's time?" she asked. Wayne nodded. He walked out onto the porch and held up a remote control. He pressed the button and several of the marked rocks blew up.

Inside, the kids all sat up in bed, startled by the explosions. They looked for their clothes and found them cleaned and folded by the door. They got dressed quickly and ran out into the hall.

Wayne was waiting there at the end of the hall. He waved them toward him. "You should all have some breakfast before she gets here," Wayne said.

"Before who gets here?" Mary asked.

"Granny Bael, of course," Wayne said. "Come on, you'll need to eat for strength to face her down."

"What?" Jemma asked.

"I'll explain the plan while you're eating eggs and bacon," Wayne said and walked away toward the kitchen.

"Tuggville sucks," Teek said with slumped shoulders as he walked toward breakfast. He looked at Mary and winked. "But it definitely has its perks."

She blushed and held his hand as they walked into the kitchen.

22

TRAP

Granny approached the bank and smiled at the man in the suit cowering inside behind the teller window. She walked through the large plate glass window, shattering it even as pieces melted in midair and fell to the ground like molten raindrops.

The man stood up suddenly and held up his hands.

"Please—don't burn me! I know where they are!" the man gibbered.

"Oh, do tell," Granny said.

"I run the loan department," the man said. "Wayne Partridge, Mary's uncle, has a ranch out east on 103. That must be where they've run to."

Granny paused and closed her eyes. She nodded her head and smiled. "Yes, I don't know how I couldn't see it before. It's right there," Granny said. She opened her eyes.

"You're not going to burn me are you?" the man asked, wincing at the fiery visage of Granny Bael staring him down.

"Of course not," Granny replied soothingly. "You've provided me the answer I need." She floated out through the large plate window frame and turned back to him. "But you're a greedy and selfish traitor to your people, so I'm afraid I'll have to bury you under the rubble of this bank," she cackled and destroyed the walls of the bank with shattering explosions of fiery brilliance. The bank toppled down on top of the loan officer in seconds even as the adjacent buildings went up in flames.

"I have what I need," Granny announced to the remaining survivors in the town square. "Now, you can all die!" With that, an eruption of flame from Granny swept through the town, burning everything in the town square to ash, incinerating all the occupants instantly.

At the library a few hundred yards away from the encircled town square, the torrent of fire and ash from the sudden destruction of the center of Tuggville burst through the windows of the building, knocking Murphy back into the stacks of books. The building and its contents caught on fire like so much kindling. He struggled to roll over and crawl out the door, but the smoke, flames, and his injuries prevented him from getting more than a few feet. He succumbed and died just inches away from the exit.

The wave of fire swept across the town, lighting every building and every tree within a mile on fire. Townspeople escaped the inferno if they could, but running from the buildings just exposed them to the burning trees and utility poles on the streets. Few in that central location survived to see the sun rise.

Granny moved through the burning wasteland with a look of glee until she reached the end of it and saw the approaching dawn. She scowled at the waning darkness.

"I'll not be denied!" she screeched and flew towards the edge of town. The accompanying wake of flames left a melted trail in the road and burned the grass and trees on either side of the route.

Wayne looked at the burning town through his binoculars and spotted the flaming figure moving swiftly down the state road toward the ranch. He turned and walked inside.

The kids were just finishing their meal at the table. Mary studied a piece of paper as she put the last piece of bacon in her mouth and chewed on it. She looked up at her mother who leaned against the refrigerator watching them eat.

"So this is why you made me learn Latin?" Mary asked. Her mother smiled and shrugged her shoulders.

"We'd do it if we had the strength," Wayne said. "But it's up to you kids. She's almost here. Remember, she needs to see you go into the barn. But be quick about it, you're not protected until you're inside."

They all got up from the table and Teek saluted. Everyone rolled their eyes.

"Go!" Wayne shouted and the kids quickly moved to the back door. Mary stopped and hugged her mom. "What about you?" Mary asked her mom.

"If everything goes right, she'll chase you and be trapped. If it doesn't..." Her mother trailed off as she looked over at Wayne. "Well, we technically don't have much time left on this earth anyway. Just try your best."

Mary clenched her teeth and nodded. She had a grim smile on her face as she turned away from them and followed her friends.

As Mary stepped outside the door, a jet of flame flew just over her head and she quickly ducked. Granny Bael entered the gravel road and tried to hit the fleeing kids. Mary ran after the others as they disappeared into the barn. The outside of the barn was covered by symbols similar to the ones on the car, fence, and rocks.

As Granny approached the barn she sent a torrent of flame at the building, but it was buffered back by an invisible barrier. "You can't hide in there forever!" Granny screeched. She approached the building where the kids had gone in and noticed a gap in the barrier there. She hesitated at the threshold and looked around.

"Chicken shit Granny Bael—afraid of her own shadow!" Teek hollered from inside. Granny scowled and entered the building. Interior walls created a kind of maze inside the barn.

"You'll burn slow, little children! I'll make sure the agony is drawn out as long as possible!" Granny emerged into a circular room and she saw Mary and Jemma looking at her through clear plastic walls with symbols drawn on them. "That won't save you!" Granny cackled.

Jemma pulled on a rope and the floor under Granny slid open revealing a barrel directly beneath her with a dark interior.

"*Captionem flamma daemoniorum!*" Mary screamed and a vortex of energy swirled inside the tar coated barrel. A torrent of blue energy swept up and around Granny Bael. It sucked her down inside the barrel. Waiting on the basement level of the floor, Teek slammed the lid down on top of the barrel and Dom hit it with a sledgehammer, securing it in place. They stepped away quickly.

"*Sigillum in aeternum!*" Mary chanted as she reached her hands up to the sky. The building quaked as lightning flashed in the sky and shot down at the barrel, sealing the edge of the lid.

"No!" Granny Bael screamed into the ether. Her scream echoed through the room and then everything went silent. A circle carved out around the barrel was filled with salt. Dom stood outside the circle and scowled at the barrel.

"That's for Uncle Howard," Dom said.

A knothole on the side of the barrel oozed black goo and a single eyeball appeared.

"Your uncle cried for mercy before I killed him. Pissed his pants too," Granny Bael cackled in a muffled voice.

Dom reached for a pitchfork set against the wall and Teek rushed to his side, grabbing his arm.

"Poor Teek, doesn't realize he's the bastard son of Elbert Dawkins, just like his half sister Jemma," Granny continued.

"Shut up, you lying bitch!" Teek shouted.

"Poor Dom, left with just your father after I cooked your mother at the hospital, her flesh fell off her bones as she screamed your name... and you weren't there for her!" Granny screeched and laughed.

"Dom, no!" Jemma shouted, but it was too late.

Teek's will faltered and he didn't stop Dom from plunging

the pitchfork into the exposed eye of Granny. The pitchfork stuck fast into the side of the barrel.

Granny screeched and then laughed as fire flew up the handle and engulfed Dom's arms. Dom kicked the barrel away and tried to put out the fire on his arms. Teek tried to pat the fire out as well. Neither of them noticed the barrel as it cracked open and Granny crawled out of the remains and flared to life with a bright yellow flame.

"Look out!" Jemma and Mary screamed, but it was too late. Granny Bael lit up Teek and Dom like medieval torches. The boys struggled for only a few seconds before their lifeless bodies fell to the floor.

Jemma and Mary pushed open the plastic walls and fled the barn. Granny Bael cackled and laughed as she shot flame up through the roof of the barn. Burned pieces of the roof and framing pelted the ground around them as they ran. Before they could reach the house, another jet of flame hit the one story building and it went up in flames quickly. Fire erupted from within the building, instantly killing anyone inside.

"Mom!" Mary screamed as she fell to her knees. Jemma stopped and pulled her friend to her feet. Mary stumbled along after her, but she moved as if all the energy had been sapped from her body. Jemma dragged her toward the car and another jet of flame knocked them to the ground. Mary fell into the drainage ditch just on the other side of the gravel drive. Jemma looked over at her just for a moment before she glanced back and saw Granny advancing on her.

Jemma scrambled to her feet and got into the car. The keys were still in the ignition and she started the car quickly.

She faced Granny approaching the car. An explosion of fire engulfed the car, but it stayed intact and didn't catch fire. Jemma screamed until she realized she wasn't burning to death. The symbols on the car protected her for the moment. She put the car in reverse and slammed her foot on the accelerator, spraying Granny with a shower of gravel, driving the fire demon backward to escape the assault.

The car moved down the drive quickly. As the flames and smoke cleared, Jemma could see behind her again. She backed onto the state highway and drove away from Tuggville as fast as the car would go.

23
SPECIAL

As Jemma approached the junction to the interstate, the car began to smoke. Flames appeared from under the hood. Jemma stopped the car and jumped out. The wards had prevented much of the fire from getting to the car, but the symbols protecting the tires had worn away and fire had spread from them to the rest of the vehicle. The damage simply became too much for the car to survive.

As Jemma ran toward the interstate, a big passenger bus rambled down the road. It passed the burning car and Jemma waved frantically at the bus. The driver stopped the bus and opened the door.

"Are you all right?" the driver asked as Jemma climbed into the bus.

"Just drive as fast as you can away from here!" Jemma said as she looked behind them and saw a glowing figure moving toward the junction from Tuggville. "Hurry!"

"We're about to get on the interstate," the driver replied.

"We'll be going plenty fast. You in trouble with the law or something?"

"I wish it was that," Jemma said. "Please, just go!"

"Okay, sit down and get comfortable. It's a bit of a hike to the next stop." The driver started the bus up and Jemma realized the back of the bus had no windows. She couldn't see where Granny Bael was anymore. She gripped the seat in front of her and squeezed her eyes shut. The faces of her friends flashed in her mind. They were all gone. Everyone was gone. Maybe her mom and brother and sister were still alive, but everyone else was gone.

The bus pulled onto the interstate and Jemma looked back at the junction. Granny passed the car and was nearly behind them. Jemma stood up.

"Please! You have to go faster!" she screamed.

"Calm down," the driver replied and then looked in the rearview mirror at the flaming figure following the bus. "What the hell?"

The driver slammed his foot on the accelerator and the bus lurched forward, quickly gaining speed as it belched out a thick cloud of black smoke behind it. The small number of passengers shouted in surprise at the jolt. Two of them popped their heads up from where they'd been slumbering.

The interstate was empty in both directions as the bus accelerated to well beyond the speed limit. On the bus, the passengers screamed in terror as a burning demon appeared to fly alongside the bus on the driver's side. Granny Bael shot forward in front of the bus and then turned back and flew straight into the driver's windshield, shattering the glass and bathing the terrified driver in a fountain of flame. The bus veered off the road, hit the drainage ditch and flipped over several times before coming to rest on its wheels once more. The collision ejected Granny Bael from the bus, but she was unharmed.

Inside the bus, Jemma picked herself up in the aisle among the other passengers. The shattered bits of her necklace fell to the floor and everything went dark.

Granny Bael floated down to the front of the bus once more and, to her surprise, the top of the bus lifted off of its own accord and fell to the side. Jemma floated in front of her in the center aisle, several feet off the floor of the bus, her head thrown back and her eyes completely white. Granny cocked her head curiously.

"This girl is under my protection. She is mine," a deep voice rumbled through the air. Granny looked around in confusion.

"What is this trickery?" Granny Bael asked.

"Witch, if you wish to keep your earthly shell, you must accept the vengeance you have found and move on."

"You have no right to her!" Granny wailed.

"She's been mine since birth," the voice responded calmly. "Her soul was surrendered in a fair pact."

"You won't deny me my vengeance!"

"Leave now or perish," the voice commanded. Granny Bael shrank back for just a moment before her entire essence flared brightly.

"No!" Granny Bael screamed and rushed toward Jemma.

Jemma's arms rose up and everything within fifty feet of

her exploded into tiny fragments. The ground was littered with flaming bits of bus, passengers and the still moving, flaming bits and pieces of Granny Bael. Granny's body attempted to coalesce once more as it had before, but this time it couldn't. Granny's flesh shuddered for a moment before all the bits stopped moving and the fires went out, leaving tiny smoking pieces of flesh, bone and hair behind.

Jemma floated a short distance away from the flaming wreckage and landed softly on the ground. She lay down with her eyes closed. She breathed quietly, at rest as the light wounds on her head from the accident still glistened with blood.

Moments later she convulsed as she woke up in a panic. She sat up slowly and looked around her. She stood up, held her head and looked around.

"Where's the bus?" she whispered.

24
REBIRTH

The ashes of the office building at the cement plant moved and fell away as a skeletal arm pushed up through the soft debris. As it grasped the top layer of ash, the blackened bone turned white. Muscle and sinew laced itself up and down the bone until a fully recognizable arm began to grow a thin layer of wrinkled skin.

After a few minutes, the figure dug itself completely out of the ash and a fully intact Elbert Dawkins arose from the wreckage and cracked his neck. He was naked and wrinkly, but every bit as healthy as the moment before Granny Bael had attempted to cremate him alive just hours ago. He sniffed and looked around. No one else was at the plant and he chuckled. He walked across the parking lot and climbed into his long black SUV. He started it up and drove away.

Elbert observed the columns of black smoke rising from across the town beyond the veil of trees, but appeared untroubled by the destruction. He actually laughed and smiled as he drove on. Ten minutes later, he pulled into the circle drive in front of his estate. He stepped out of the vehicle and strode up the flight of stairs to meet his startled butler walking out the door.

"Owens, get me a fresh set of clothing, something durable and functional, then alert Simmons and Flack—we have some work to do," Elbert said as he strode forward through the estate to his private study. He picked up the phone and dialed it quickly.

"Mayor Brown, glad to find you've survived our little fire demon episode. I need you to assemble the town council at my house this evening at 5 P.M. sharp," Elbert said. He frowned at the response. "The town's recovery is exactly what this meeting is about. It will recover according my plans. Is that clear?" Again Elbert frowned and then sighed. "Is she still burning everything up?" Elbert waited and nodded. "Then she's been neutralized somehow or she'd be back ensuring everything was torched. Get the council here. I'm not going to ask again," Elbert said firmly and hung up the phone. "Idiot."

Owens appeared with a pressed set of overalls, underwear, blue plaid flannel shirt, socks and a pair of work boots. Elbert handed the flannel shirt back to Owens.

"Plain shirt, beige I think. I'm not a lumberjack," Elbert said. "But get me the boys first."

"As you wish, Mister Dawkins," Owens said and bowed his head slightly. The impeccably dressed butler rushed from the room as Elbert got dressed.

Two well-muscled men, one blonde and one brunette, in dark suits and sunglasses, entered the room a few moments later. Elbert finished putting on the work boots and stood up.

"War room, now," he said and started walking. The men followed silently, always checking out the surrounding area as they walked. They took in everything as they moved even though nothing had changed since they walked in the room seconds ago.

Elbert strode quickly across the vast building. He entered a large ballroom with a map of Tuggville plastered on one long wall. He pointed at the map.

"Update it," he said simply. Owens arrived with a plain beige shirt and Elbert put it on as he watched.

The two men went to a side table with drawers and pulled out a set of pins with different colored flags. They set about updating the map, red flags for areas still on fire, black for areas damaged beyond repair and yellow for damage that was deemed repairable. They consulted a notebook and went back and forth with a ladder updating the status of the entire town. There was a clear trail of destruction from The District leading up to the cement plant and back down through a wide swath of houses until the area around the town square was colored black. Earthquake damage was also noted.

Elbert's eyes scanned over the entire town taking in the damage. He walked up and pointed to the grocery store.

"Deering? Did he survive?" Elbert asked.

The men consulted their notebooks and shook their head. "He's deceased," the blonde man said.

"Shame," Elbert said folding his arms and sniffing. "He was a good man. Visionary."

He glanced north of the grocery and noted total

destruction for one of the buildings there.

"My daughter-in-law and grandchildren?"

"Sorry, sir. They're deceased. Except for Jemma. She's in the wind."

"No need for sorrow. Just missed opportunities for exploitation. Shame to lose those resources. We'll locate Jemma soon enough. Or perhaps she'll make her appointment here Saturday?" Elbert chuckled at his own joke.

Elbert studied the map for a while longer and then raised his eyebrows. He pointed at a small house showing earthquake damage.

"Tell me," he said simply.

The men reviewed their notebooks. The darker haired man nodded and spoke. "Residence of Abigail Partridge, cottage construction, appears several trees fell on the house, mostly crushing it."

"Fire damage?"

The man shook his head. "The house just shows collapse. The trees that fell on it have some char marks at the broken trunk ends, but they were healthy trees and didn't spread any fire to the structure."

"Emergency response?"

"The house has not been visited by emergency personnel. Those that weren't killed in the rampage are dealing with the fire around the town square."

"Excellent. Let's go retrieve a body. Hopefully she's still alive. I have a score to settle."

25

RETURN

Jemma stumbled up the gravel path. The ranch house was nothing but burning cinders. The barn behind it had collapsed into a bouquet of jagged charcoal spears. Mary, though, had pulled herself out of the drainage ditch and sat next to it holding her head.

Jemma sat down next to her. Mary looked over at her and Jemma saw the flash burn on the side of Mary's face. It was red and probably hurt like hell, but it would eventually peel and heal like a sunburn. The trickle of blood from beneath her hairline was more concerning.

"I have a headache," Mary said and looked back down into the ditch.

"I need to go into town to see if the rest of my family survived," Jemma said. She stood up. Mary reached a hand up to her and Jemma helped her stand as well. Mary winced and wobbled a little, but took a deep breath and blinked her bloodshot, red-rimmed eyes.

"Maybe you should drive," Mary said. Jemma chuckled.

"Your aunt's car didn't survive."

"Hmm," Mary responded. She looked at the ranch house and sighed. "At least they're at peace. Uncle Wayne's truck should be behind the house if it survived."

They stumbled around the burned out house and saw the truck sitting far enough away from the house to not catch fire, but it was covered with soot and a small amount of charred splinters. They both walked to the driver's side and Jemma opened the door. The keys dangled from the ignition switch.

"Uncle Wayne always thought ahead," Mary said. She sniffed a little, but she was all cried out. She'd grieved while Jemma was walking back from the interstate. "I'm not sure we'll find anyone we care about left in town."

"I have to try," Jemma said. She helped Mary climb into the truck. Mary scooted over and Jemma climbed in after her. She started the truck and pulled around the house carefully giving it a wide berth.

They carefully drove up the gravel road pockmarked with scorched earth. The truck rumbled to a stop at the end as Jemma looked both ways. The state road was empty. She mused that it matched her soul as she glanced in the rearview mirror at the collapsed barn. She wasn't sure she had anything left to live for.

Elbert stepped up to the outer salt ring surrounding Abigail's cottage. He looked left at his blonde haired companion, Simmons, who stood by holding a pickaxe. He gave Simmons a nod and the pickaxe swung down, breaking up the plastic enclosed salt.

Elbert stepped back a few paces and stood next to his other enforcer, the dark haired Flack.

"Is this really necessary?" Flack asked.

"Just eliminating any last booby traps she may have laid in place. You never can trust a witch. My father taught me that."

"Are you referring to Granny Bael?" Flack asked.

"She was never supposed to come back after she was burned at the stake. She lied to my father and he overplayed his hand. She was tricky, I'll give her that. But, I can sense she's finally left this earth. Nothing to stand in my way now."

"Even this witch here?" Flack pointed at the cottage where a strand of blonde hair could be seen sticking out from under the rubble.

"She was never a danger, only a nuisance," Elbert smiled as a few more workmen arrived and began clearing rubble carefully. "This retrieval is solely for my amusement."

If Flack was disturbed by the implication, you couldn't see it on his face which remained impassive.

As Simmons brought down the pickaxe on the final salt circle, there was a bright flash where the tip of the tool struck the ground. Simmons was blown back from the cottage, flying through the air and striking a tree. Simmons lay motionless where he finally landed. Elbert sighed.

"Never trust a witch," he said as he watched the workmen pull Abigail from the rubble and carry her away from the cottage. They all left the area, abandoning the dead Simmons where he lay on the ground.

Jemma and Mary stopped the truck a few blocks away from her house. Power poles and lines blocked the road. Smoke rose in the distance. Several structures had burned through the night. It didn't appear as if any emergency vehicles had made it this far.

"You think you'll be all right here?" Jemma asked. "I'm going to walk to my house."

Mary nodded and rested her head against the passenger side window. She closed her eyes and sighed. She vaguely wondered if she'd ever sleep again even as exhaustion caused her to fall asleep nearly immediately.

Jemma got out of the car and carefully stepped through the front yards that seemed clear. She didn't see any power lines in the yards at all, so she felt confident that way was safe. As she moved along the street, she noted the absence of any people in the houses. It was eerie hearing nothing but the wind rustling the leaves overhead. Even the power lines were silent. Jemma doubted they were even live anymore, but she wasn't going to test them first hand.

She stopped in front of the Jackson's house and cocked her head. Their big hairy dog, Alvin, was always barking whenever anyone walked by. He was silent. She wondered if he'd simply escaped or had passed away in the night. It was like walking through a ghost town.

She stepped over a red bike sitting in the Jackson's front yard and turned the corner. As her eyes landed on the house at the end of the cul-de-sac, she stopped dead in her tracks and sat down on the ground. Her house and the two on either side of it were charred wood frame skeletons. Wisps of smoke rose from them into the crisp morning air.

The emptiness she felt in her soul began to hurt. The tears threatened to burst from her eyes but she shook her head viciously. She had to be sure they were gone.

Jemma stood up again and walked slowly toward the house, her feet dragging as if through thick mud. Her mom's car was still intact; it had been parked on the street, not in the driveway. Her dad liked to use the garage and always yelled at Diedre if she parked her car there because he couldn't pull in. That was likely because she wasn't entirely sober when she drove and couldn't park straight. This little quirk had saved it from the fire that spread through the houses behind it.

She walked up to the car and glanced over the hood into the front lawn. She shut her eyes and turned her head. There were three smoking corpses in the grass. A medium sized one she took to be her mom and two smaller ones she knew immediately were her brother and sister. The smell of burned flesh rose into the air as well and Jemma gagged. She blinked her eyes quickly and opened the car door. She reached under the seat and grabbed the envelope her mom kept her liquor money in. She stuffed it into her pocket and fled.

Abigail opened her eyes and noted a small trickle of light coming in through a high window. As her eyes adjusted to the light, a sickening dread filled her mind. She instantly recognized the dusty black walls of the dungeon beneath Elbert Dawkins' mansion. She'd been here before and the memories were something she'd suppressed for a long time.

She shuddered as they flooded back into her head.

Elbert had invited her to celebrate the capture and encasement of Granny Bael, something he'd participated in silently and with just his brother while creating her sarcophagus. Abigail hadn't thought to check with the others to see if they'd been invited as well. Howard was mourning the loss of his brother, so she didn't bug him about it. She figured he probably wouldn't come anyway. She didn't realize she was the lone attendee until she sat in the ballroom looking at the town map on the wall. They'd dragged her screaming from there to this dungeon of torture and depravity.

The abuse and violation she suffered the next month under Elbert's twisted machinations had changed her forever. There was nowhere on this planet she'd rather not be than this basement chamber.

"Ah, you're awake," Elbert said smoothly as he approached from the darkness. Had he always been there or had she just not noticed him come in under the onslaught of memory overloading her brain?

"Go to hell!" Abigail said.

"Ah, you do remember our precious time together then… excellent," Elbert said with an oily air of satisfaction. "Unfortunately, you've grown older than the joyless youth I felt under me all those years ago. You've aged out of my carnal target, I'm afraid."

"What a shame," Abigail snarled back.

"Instead, I'll be enjoyed the darker side of my nature on you," Elbert said. "The violence I can only unleash in the privacy of my dungeon upon a soul who will never leave the premises alive. The freedom that can only be found when there is no need to be concerned about scars, broken bones or flayed skin."

"You're sick," Abigail accused.

"Oh you have no idea," Elbert said. "But when you're immortal, you need to maintain a diverse set of hobbies throughout the centuries to keep your sanity."

"Immortal?"

"Traded my firstborn to a very willing demon for that pleasure," Elbert said. "From knowledge I gained from none other than Granny Balsom herself, may she rest."

"Granny's dead?"

"Indeed. Got the reports back from one of my men on the outskirts of town. Strangest thing he ever saw, but Granny is no more. But, she left behind so many treasures to find."

Elbert walked over to the far corner and clicked on a single light bulb above an altar with an old book on it. He stroked the book lovingly. "I'm sure I'll find more secrets as the centuries pass, maybe even the secret to being invulnerable. Coming back from death is unpleasant at best," he said and looked at Abigail. "I don't recommend it."

He laughed heartily at his joke. Abigail just gave him a disgusted look. "Of course, eventually you will succumb to the wounds I inflict upon you. It isn't like you'll be seeing a doctor ever again. So you'll never really know the joy of eternal life. It's really quite freeing," Elbert smiled and looked up at the window which seemed to have darkened just a bit since Abigail first opened her eyes.

"Time flies," Elbert said. "I'll leave you here to ponder the joy of my return and the pain and suffering I will draw from your flesh. But, I must meet with the town leaders on rebuilding the town into a true paradise for one such as myself and similarly minded political leaders of this generation. A true Sodom and Gomorrah where the young shall provide the old and immortal with joys beyond measure and the best part is they can never leave."

Elbert walked up a flight of steps to a heavy wooden door and turned to look at her from the top.

"Your niece and my delightfully illegitimate daughter will be the first servants to my whims in this new era," Elbert laughed. "I thought you'd enjoy pondering that as well."

Abigail jumped to her feet and felt the shackles around her ankles. She looked down in despair at long chains leading to an eyebolt in the wall behind her. Elbert laughed again and closed the door.

Abigail stood there for several minutes in shock. She'd been so careful to put up the protections around her cottage to keep this bastard away. She looked at the fading light in the window and sighed. The lone light bulb in the corner caught her eye. He hadn't turned it off. Granny Balsom's book sat there on the altar. Abigail smiled.

26
RETRIBUTION

Elbert strode down the long hall until he reached his study. He looked toward the front entrance of the estate.

"Owens!" Elbert shouted.

"Yes sir," Owens replied as he emerged from the foyer.

"Have the chef cook me up a steak and serve it with all the fixings in the ballroom in fifteen minutes. I want to eat before the guests arrive," Elbert said.

"Chef Andre died in the town square last night, sir," Owens replied. "Shall I fetch you something from the pantry instead?"

"Right, we'll need to replace him. Add that to the schedule. A sandwich and a few pickle spears ought to suffice, then."

"Very good, sir."

"Oh, and a bowl of wet dog food for our guest downstairs. We should spoil her on her first day with us." Elbert paused for a moment. "Best serve it after I've convened the meeting upstairs. You may want to take a stick with you to ensure obedience."

"Of course," Owens said and bowed before turning to fetch the food.

Elbert sat down and looked through the books on his desk.

Abigail stretched toward the book, but her fingers were still inches away. The chain shackled to her feet was just short enough to keep her from the altar. She screamed at the ceiling. She grabbed the thick chain and yanked on it.

She fell backward on her ass when the eyebolt pulled loose from the wall and clanged to a rest several feet away. The shackles had been in place since before she was last incarcerated here and never received maintenance in all the years since. Her eyes darted to the door and she waited for a moment before deciding her captor hadn't heard anything. Abigail thrilled at the unforeseen drawback for her jailer that soundproofing the dungeon brought.

She clamored to her feet and shuffled to the altar, still dragging the chain connected to her shackles. When she reached the book, she opened it up and started searching. She stopped when she reached a page that looked familiar. She recognized the text and symbols from the days just before Granny Balsom had been imprisoned. This was all copied into the notebook that had mysteriously appeared in her locker. Had Elbert slipped it into her locker to help them trap Granny Bael? Why hadn't he used it himself?

"He doesn't know how," she whispered. "Then whose

book is this?"

She leafed through the book and frowned. While she recognized the pages that she used to imprison Granny Balsom, she didn't see anything apparent that would help with her predicament. She looked for some kind of incantation to release a lock or maybe teleportation or something outlandish like that. Her eyes fell upon a spell that she was something similar to what she'd been preparing on her own to banish Granny Balsom. It would have the opposite effect, though. A summoning spell of sorts... the same one that gave Granny Balsom her fiery persona in the first place. She frowned. Had the Dawkins' brought the fire demon forth themselves? Perhaps they thought to bend it to their will and it backfired.

Abigail studied the spell and leafed through more of the book. She found something that could make it a little different, but she'd have to get help from a most unlikely source. She opened the drawers built into the altar and located some old matches, candles and a bowl. She stuffed the book inside the drawer and closed it. She looked around the room and found the utility sink along another wall. She shuddered as she recalled Elbert waterboarding her for hours on end just for the pleasure of her fear of drowning. She shuffled over and filled the bowl with water. She set it next to the altar and looked around in the drawers for other items.

A single, long gray hair was tucked into a corner of one drawer. It was too long to be Elbert's. She examined it and something told her who it belonged to. "Always trust that little voice," she whispered.

She found some chalk and drew a pentagram on the floor. She set the candles up around it and then sat down in the center with the bowl of water. It took some extra concentrating to put the ankle shackles out of her mind, but eventually Abigail fell into a trance. She controlled her breathing and steadied her mind. She spoke words ancient and eldritch, piercing the veil between life and death. Abigail's mind treaded into a world she swore she would never venture into.

Floating in the water in front of her was that single strand of gray hair. Abigail hoped it belonged to Granny Balsom; otherwise, she was searching for the wrong entity and may never find her.

Granny Balsom, Abigail's mind called out gently into the ether. Abigail issued the call softly and repeatedly. At first, there was no answer, just a low ethereal wind whispering through the nebulous caverns of Abigail's mind. The passage of time was hard to judge within the trance. Abigail wasn't sure how much time had passed before she felt Granny's presence come near.

What do you want? Granny spoke the words crankily.

I mean no harm, Abigail replied.

Then why do you interrupt my peace? I seem to remember you wishing it for me… a long time ago.

I need your help, Abigail said simply.

Why should I help you? I know you… you're the one who trapped me in that infernal barrel, Granny accused. *I should leave you to suffer without my aid.*

I offer you my body as a vessel for your vengeance,

Abigail said.

What? Granny snapped and the ethereal wind picked up in intensity. *What kind of trick is this?*

Elbert Dawkins still lives, Abigail said. *He has gained immortality.*

Ugh, Granny groaned. *So that's what the demon traded for.*

He has the power of regeneration, Abigail said. *I don't think we can destroy him, but that is the limit of his power.*

Elwin made a mockery of my research. I should have never shared any of my secrets with him. And then he entrusted it all to that murderous thug Elbert and his scheming brother who never seems to be around anymore. I couldn't feel Alex anywhere these last ten years. But, we can certainly make Elbert suffer, Granny surmised. *What of the others, the children?*

I can't let you harm them. You've destroyed most of the town as it is. Remove Elbert Dawkins from the equation and I think Tuggville will disappear altogether. Isn't that enough? Abigail maintained a quiet, serene tone, but she was furious at the carnage that had befallen the town at Granny's hands. Even now, she was second guessing her deal with the devil.

It will have to do, Granny replied. *Elbert Dawkins must pay for eternity as I have.*

Then I welcome you in, Granny Balsom. Let's take this fight to the real evil in Tuggville.

Granny merged with Abigail and everything went white with pain.

Abigail awoke on the floor of the dungeon. She looked up at the sole window and saw it had grown much darker. The sun struggled to light up the sky with its last rays.

Abigail sat up and looked around. The candles had burned down a bit and the melted wax merged with the stone floor.

It's time to lose these shackles, Granny's voice said in her head. The shackles glowed red and then white hot. Abigail felt someone else will her hands to grasp the white hot metal and pull the shackles off her ankles. She felt only a dull pain as she grasped something that appeared to be heated to hundreds of degrees if not thousands.

As she stood up, Abigail marveled at the fiery color of her skin as she held up her hand and looked at it.

Enough gawking, Granny's voice commanded and Abigail felt herself walk forward. She willed her body to stop and she stopped walking.

Do you want this to happen or what? Granny growled.

It will happen on my terms, Abigail answered firmly. *I give you free reign to destroy Elbert, but I'll decide if you need to hold back. I just needed to make sure I was still in control.*

Don't be naïve. Other people are going to die, Granny said. *He has allies, protectors. They will need to be eliminated or they can aid in his recovery. Besides, I've seen what he did to you; I don't know why you'd want to hold back anything at this point.*

"Good point," Abigail said aloud. "Let's go burn some things."

Elbert walked into the large conference room on the second floor of the estate. Eleven men sat around the table and looked up as he walked in. Flack walked in after Elbert and took up a position next to the door, closing it behind him.

"Gentlemen, let's talk about our plans for the new and revised Tuggville, which we shall heretofore rename Dawkins," Elbert said.

"It's a little presumptuous that we'd want to change the town name," a middle aged man with glasses and thinning black hair said. He sat at the head of the table.

"How are you going to rebuild without my money?" Elbert asked.

The men looked around at each other and sighed.

"Now, Dawkins will be rebranded. It will become a resort of sorts for the wealthy and powerful. Nothing within city limits will be off the table. No foul act or debauchery will be out of bounds," Elbert said.

"Well, since you banned churches twenty years ago, there certainly won't be many to object. But there will be various townspeople who won't agree with the new direction," a blonde haired man in a tan suit replied. He kicked his feet up on the table. "Not that there are many left. Granny Bael seemed to take quite a few out of the equation during her rampage."

"Any objectors will be the first volunteers subject to visiting dignitaries' depravities," Elbert said as he walked around the table. "I already have law enforcement looking the other way in every county and at the state level. I've even got a few Senators under retainer to help keep our little experiment away from scrutiny. I suspect a few of them will come and partake as well."

Abigail entered the hallway on the first floor and rounded the corner, startling Owens. He dropped the book he was holding, a tome of arcane rituals Granny recognized from her collection.

"Just studying up, I see, Owens," Abigail said. Faster than he should've been able to, Owens pulled a switchblade from his pocket and rushed Abigail. She grabbed his attacking hand with a swiftness that made Owens gasp. With her other hand, she grabbed him around the throat. The old man struggled but couldn't escape her grasp.

"I remember you, Owens," Abigail said. Her hand holding his knife arm began to glow red. Smoke rose from his arm and he dropped the switchblade.

"Master will make you pay!" Owens croaked as he tried to gather air.

Abigail pushed him up against the wall. "First, you're going to pay, dear Owens. Pay for helping him strap me down when I was a teenager, for gathering his tools of torture, for supplying him with the drugs to keep me sedated." Abigail's voice grew with each accusation. "How many others did you help him torture?"

"A... delightful... number," Owens struggled to get out through his constricted windpipe.

"Enjoy hell, bastard," Abigail hissed. Her hand around Owens' throat glowed white hot and the skin on his neck began to bubble and smoke. A strangled scream erupted from Owens throat for a moment before the tissue burned through and his vocal cords shriveled up to burnt cinders. Fire engulfed his head and shoulders and he went limp.

The charred skull fell from his shoulders as his body dropped to the floor.

"What about this Granny Bael? She burned down half the town, for chrissakes," said a portly red haired man sitting in the middle of the table.

"Well, Granny Bael has been eliminated. Destroyed. She's no longer of any concern," Elbert replied as he reached the head of the table and put his hands on the shoulders of the middle-aged man with glasses.

The door burst open, nearly hitting Flack, who ducked out of the way as the headless burning corpse of Owens landed smack dab in the middle of the conference table, exploding on impact, showering those men sitting nearby with flecks of burning flesh and boiling hot bodily fluids. Flack jumped into the doorway, gun drawn, and didn't even have time to pull the trigger before a fireball connected with him, sending him over the table to hit the back wall with a loud crack. His burning body fell to the floor and lay still.

Everyone except Elbert got up from the table and pressed themselves into the corners of the room trying to escape as Abigail walked into the room, her body aflame, hair flowing up into air buoyed by the heated winds swirling around her.

"Elbert," Abigail said. "Did you miss us?"

"What a nuisance," Elbert replied.

"Is this the town council, come to your beck and call?" Abigail said as she looked around the room. "I recognize them all, spouting your will at the council meetings. It's a shame the good sheriff didn't make it to your little boys' club gathering."

"Seems our local law enforcement was caught up in a free-for-all in the town square last night," Elbert replied dryly. "Perhaps you recall something of his whereabouts?"

"Oh, Granny does. Oh dear, I never realized you could do that with a molten flagpole." Abigail's eyes got wide. "She does have an imagination."

"You should give this up. You know you can't kill me," Elbert said.

"We're still working out the kinks on how to deal with that. But," Abigail smiled, "your immortality doesn't extend to everyone in this room, does it?"

The blonde haired man held up his hands and said "Wait!"

But it was too late. The room filled with an inferno that burned everything in it to a cinder within seconds.

27
RECKONING

Jemma jerked awake in the truck while Mary continued to snore away. She looked at her face in the rearview mirror. Even in the fading sunlight, she saw the streaks under her eyes from the tears. She wiped them away and started the truck. That was enough to wake Mary.

"Well," Jemma said. "I don't have anything left in town to stay for. I have to assume my father's dead. He wanted me to leave anyway."

"Can we check on my aunt?" Mary asked.

"I don't see why not," Jemma replied and turned the car around to head to Abigail's cottage.

"I'm sorry I wasn't awake when you returned," Mary said. "Was it bad?"

"I'd like to think they died quickly," Jemma replied. "What I don't get is, why am I still alive?"

"You don't remember what happened?"

Jemma shook her head. "Bus ran off the road and... I

don't remember anything after that. I can't even remember if I hit my head or something. I just woke up and the bus and everything in it was in tiny bits and pieces all around me. Oh, and that nice necklace is gone. So much for that calm peace I experienced all too briefly."

"Maybe Granny Bael blew up in the sunlight?"

"Naw, it's gotta be something else," Jemma said. "I feel like the answer is in my head but whenever I try to think about it, the memory just slides away."

"You must've hit your head. Trust me, I know the feeling," Mary said, touching her own head where the blood had caked dry.

They drove on in silence, reflecting on everything that had disappeared in a single day. Friends, family, and large chunks of the town they'd grown up in. The feeling of helplessness and despair hung heavy in the truck cab.

After a few detours around downed power lines, they finally reached Abigail's cottage. They parked the truck where Abigail's sedan had been parked. The lights illuminated the cascade of trees that had fallen on the small house. The rest of the area was partially illuminated by a full moon rising into the night sky. Without the cloud cover, the chill in the night air deepened.

"I don't think emergency crews have made it here," Mary said. "Maybe Aunt Abby is still in there."

They got out of the car and approached the house, the truck still running to provide light. Jemma pointed to the left side of the house.

"There's a body!" she yelled and they both ran to it. They

slowed as they got closer and realized it wasn't Abigail. The man was face down but they could see his hands had been burned somehow. Jemma pushed the body over with her foot and gasped. Even with the burn marks on his face, she recognized him.

"That's Simmons, one of my grandfather's associates," she said. They looked at the house.

"What would they want with my aunt?" Mary asked.

They walked over and found a path cleared to the house and an area where rubble had been removed.

"We know what my grandfather would want. What if he's not dead?" Jemma asked as she squinted at the empty space in the debris.

Mary walked over and picked up the pickaxe that had been thrown free when Simmons had been electrocuted.

"If he's not dead, he's about to be," Mary stated and walked to the truck.

"You would kill someone?" Jemma asked.

Mary stopped and turned back to Jemma. "It's amazing what someone will do when they've got nothing left to lose."

Jemma watched Mary turn and walk away. Her words hit home. She was in the same spot. She ran over to Simmons body and searched through his pockets, finding a gun with a clip. She found a spare clip in his pockets and put it in her pocket. She tucked the weapon into the waistband of her jeans and ran after Mary.

The burned cadaver turned over and got to its hands and knees. The blackened skin turned pink as it regenerated. After a few minutes, the thin gray-haired head of Elbert Dawkins looked over at Abigail sitting in a torched chair, the building around her in full conflagration.

"You see," he said, smoke billowing from his mouth as his soot filled lungs expelled the noxious fumes. He paused to spit out chunks of acrid charred bits of flesh. "You can't kill me."

Abigail watched the old man rise to his feet unsteadily.

"While killing you over and over again is fun, it's getting tedious," she said. She stood up suddenly and gasped. "I remember! He probably doesn't know!"

"Don't know what?" Elbert asked. In answer, Abigail sent a fireball at Elbert, knocking him out the window into the covered pool house below. His burning body crashed through the glass roof and splashed into the heated pool. Abigail followed him out the window and floated on a column of heated air to the ground below.

Elbert popped up in the middle of the pool. He laughed. "Perhaps I'll just stay in the water where you can't hurt me?" he pondered.

Abigail put her hand to her chin, striking the pose of someone thinking deeply. "Do you really think so?" she asked and the water began to steam and boil. Elbert screamed in agony and fell beneath the water. He popped back up, screamed and dropped beneath the surface again. He slowly made his way to the edge of the pool and, after going through the dying cycle several times, managed to pull himself out of the pool.

He held his hand up and spit boiling water out of his face.

He doubled over and coughed several times. Then he fell to the pool deck and died again. After a few minutes, he sat up.

"Point taken," he said as he stood up. His naked wrinkled body shook from the cold.

"Aww, you look chilly," Abigail said and launched another fireball at Elbert, sending his burning body through the rear wall of the pool house. It struck the brick wall surrounding the back yard with an audible, wet crack. Elbert's smoking body fell to the ground again, motionless for a time.

As Elbert regenerated and began to stand up, Abigail smiled. "How many people have you killed, Elbert?" she asked.

"More than your feeble mind can calculate!" Elbert shouted.

"So we're nowhere near repaying you with a death for a death yet, are we?" Abigail said sweetly. She fired another ball of what appeared to be lava at Elbert who held up his hands as the burning liquid engulfed him. The wall behind him burst apart as the water in the concrete and bricks instantly expanded into steam.

Elbert regenerated several times and died in the molten pit as it slowly cooled. Finally, he was able to meticulously claw his way out of the fiery concoction into the woods beyond the fence. He fell again, dying with one of his feet still imbedded in the cooling liquid.

When he regenerated again, he screamed out in pain. His foot was stuck firmly in the cooled magma. He tugged at the limb repeatedly, but couldn't get it free.

Abigail walked up next to him and examined the limb stuck firmly in the blackening substance. "Can't get free?"

Abigail asked with mocking sorrow. "How does it feel to be trapped, Elbert? Trapped against your will and at the mercy of someone with *no mercy left in their soul!*" Abigail shrieked the last part and Granny Bael surfaced in full fury. "*Let me help you!*" She cackled and grabbed Elbert's trapped leg, burning it into cinders, freeing the rest of his body. Elbert collapsed on the ground from shock and died yet again. Abigail stood back and watched as the substance trapped within the magma slowly trickled out to rejoin Elbert, slowly regenerating the missing limb.

Elbert's eyes fluttered open. He laughed weakly. "I'll trap you again, Granny, and pull you and Abigail apart so I can torture her again. You have no power over me," Elbert said as he grinned.

Abigail laughed. "I'm touched, Elbert. Truly touched that you haven't realized the depth of the predicament you're in."

"What?" Elbert mocked as he stood and spread his arms wide. "Are you going to kill me again? Go for it!"

Abigail cocked her head at the old man standing in front of her and obliged, the fireball sent Elbert up into the air hundreds of feet. His burning body wasn't quite dead before it fell into the forest, striking several trees and then the ground, breaking nearly every bone in his body.

Abigail strode forward through the forest landscape, leaving a trial of burned footprints in the fallen leaves and undergrowth, but took care not to set the entire forest ablaze. She came upon Elbert's broken body as the bones reset with sickening pops and click inside the burned bag of skin. Slowly it formed a human appearance again. The skin rejuvenated and Elbert sat up again.

"You'll tire of killing me over and over again, Abigail," he said as he stood. "What then, my fiery angel? Will we patch up our differences and find carnal pleasures in our shared mutual joy of murder?"

"Over and over, Elbert?" Abigail said. "Come now. Surely, a serial killing psychopath like you can come up with a more efficient way of sending a message destined to repeat over and over again for eternity. I'm disappointed."

Elbert glanced behind him and saw an opening in the forest. He dashed away from Abigail into a clearing. He stopped midpoint when he encountered a gaping hole in the landscape barely illuminated by the moonlight overhead. He skirted around the edge and continued to make his way across the small clearing. Abigail emerged from the forest and raised her hands. A thick wall of flame encircled the meadow, blocking Elbert's path. Elbert turned back to her and raised his fist.

"Your flames can't stop an immortal," Elbert shouted and rushed into the flaming wall. He fell halfway through, dying for the umpteenth time that night.

Abigail calmly walked up to him in the depths of the flames and grabbed the dead man's ankle, pulling him back to the edge of the hole.

As Elbert regenerated again, he looked back at the hole in fear. He stood up and returned his attention to Abigail with a scowl. "I'll claw my way back out of that hole—I don't care how deep it is!"

"Surely," Abigail said with a smirk. "But how many eons of

dying and being reborn will it take for you to dig yourself out from under tons of earth and stone?"

"What?" Elbert said with a frown.

"It's time, Granny. This is our exit," Abigail said.

So be it, Granny answered.

Abigail launched herself at Elbert with a scream and they grappled just for a moment at the edge before they both fell in. A minute later, a large explosion shook the ground and the abandoned mine shaft collapsed, leaving behind a crater marked by a plume of dust that slowly settled back down onto the earth.

28

LAST CALL

As they approached the estate, Jemma slowed the truck to a crawl. Her grandfather's estate was in flames. There were no emergency vehicles in sight even though there were a bunch of cars parked in the huge semi-circle in front of the sprawling mansion.

"If he was alive, he would've made them come to save his precious estate," Jemma said.

"Best to be certain," Mary said. Her lips were taut and pale, while her furrowed brow shrunk her eyes to mere slits as she scanned the surrounding grounds for movement. She opened the glove box and pulled out a flashlight.

Jemma pulled the truck around and pointed it away from the building so they could make a quick escape if they needed to. "Hey," she said to Mary, who looked at her. Jemma turned off the truck and put the keys under the seat. "Just in case one of us doesn't make it."

"Well, you better be good and dead, because I'm not

leaving you behind otherwise," Mary said. She handed Jemma the flashlight as she grabbed the pickaxe. "I'll need two hands to wield this, I think."

Jemma smiled and picked up the gun sitting on the seat next to her. They got out of the truck and closed the doors gently. They looked into the flickering flames and couldn't discern any movement besides the occasional collapsing timber inside the structure. After glancing around the grounds in front of the estate, they walked around it to the back.

Mary stopped near the rear of the structure. An old set of stone stairs led into a basement filled with debris that still smoldered. She felt a tug in her mind. She searched the debris, but couldn't tell what drew her to the spot.

Jemma walked up next to her and looked down into the basement. "What is it?" Jemma asked.

"I'm not quite sure," Mary replied as she stepped over the remains of the building's smoking outer wall to the top of the stairs.

"Do you think someone's in there? Still alive?"

"No," Mary said. "I feel the shadow of my aunt's presence. It's like she was here... but now she isn't. I can't explain it. I need to go down there."

Jemma looked into the hole of smoking debris and felt a sense of dread. "I don't think it's safe," Jemma said.

"Neither do I," Mary replied as she stepped down to the lowest step and kicked at the charred wood, kicking up a little shower of flaming embers into the air. She used the pickaxe to push timbers out of the way as she made her way forward. She stepped carefully, trying to avoid anything that looked like it was still on fire or red hot.

Mary reached the back corner and pushed a large timber down. Smoke and burning ash flew up in the air. She turned away and backed up a few steps. When the ash settled somewhat, she looked in the corner and saw the charred remains of the altar. The drawer in the center of it glowed blue. "Jemma, do you see that?" Mary asked excitedly.

From her vantage point at the edge of the building, Jemma squinted. "I see burned stuff," Jemma replied. "Maybe you should leave it alone."

"I've come this far, I'm not leaving here without whatever it is. I think my aunt wanted me to find it."

Jemma paced nervously along the chunk of charred wall. "Well, just hurry up. Something doesn't feel right."

Mary touched the drawer and then drew her hand back quickly. The altar was still hot to the touch. She inserted the tip of the pickaxe in the edge of the drawer and pried it open. The faint blue glow around the book inside faded. Mary grabbed the book and held it up. "I got it!" she shouted.

"Now it's no longer protected," Jemma replied in a monotone voice.

"What?" Mary asked as she climbed back over the debris.

Jemma blinked her eyes and shook her head. "I said something doesn't feel right," Jemma replied and looked around. She looked at the covered pool and noticed the destruction of the roof. She walked to the side and looked through the glass at the hole in the ceiling. Mary caught up with her and looked through it as well. They both looked to the rear of the pool house and saw a hole through the building. They walked around to the rear of the pool house and followed the trail of destruction to the brick wall surrounding the estate.

"Someone had a rough night," Jemma smirked. They moved to the smoking rubble at the rear wall. Mary bent down and put her hand near the smooth, cooling surface of the molten substance.

"That's still warm. Is this fresh?" Mary asked.

"But Granny's dead, isn't she?" Jemma asked. She reflexively felt for the necklace Abigail had given her earlier and made a sour face when she remembered it was gone.

"Fuck, I hope so," Mary said. She motioned with the pickaxe resting on her shoulder. "This isn't going to do shit against her."

They carefully climbed around the smoking debris to the forest behind it. They looked at the footprints burned into the forest floor.

"Maybe we let her take care of business and get the hell out of here," Jemma said.

"We wouldn't get far," Mary replied.

Jemma, a voice whispered.

Jemma whirled around with the gun and looked wildly at the surrounding woods with the flashlight. "Did you hear that?" she asked.

"Hear what?" Mary replied. She put the book down and lifted the pickaxe up, ready for anything. She looked around at the forest. There was no movement or sound outside of the smoldering mansion wreckage crackling behind her.

"He's alive," Jemma said.

"How the fuck is that possible?" Mary replied. "Granny Bael can kill anything and everything."

"I don't know, but maybe we need to finish the job. Maybe that's our purpose."

Jemma followed the burned steps tracking through the thin blanket of leaves and undergrowth. She could smell the burned foliage and it made her nose twitch. She maintained course until she saw a flicker of flames through the trees ahead and emerged into the clearing, stepping on a burned circle around the perimeter that had mostly gone out, but still flared up in places. Mary stepped out onto the burned grass and it crunched beneath her feet.

Jemma, the voice said, louder this time, but Jemma could tell it was in her mind and not her ears. She held up her hand to Mary.

"Who's there?" Jemma asked. Mary raised her pickaxe.

Jemma—dig me out, the voice she now recognized as her grandfather said.

"Where are you?" Jemma asked.

At the— the voice stopped and Jemma heard a scream of agony in her mind causing her to flinch. The voice went silent.

"I heard him in my head," Jemma said. The revulsion was hard to disguise.

"I didn't hear anything," Mary replied.

"Lucky you," Jemma said as she walked around the clearing and noticed the depression in the center. She pointed to the crater. "Stay away from there. That looks recently disturbed. There's dirt and rocks mixed in with the grass." Jemma stayed at the perimeter and kept walking around.

Bottom of the mine shaft, Elbert's voice rang in her head clearly again.

"Trapped?" Jemma said unable to contain the glee she felt.

Dig me out or— Again Elbert's voice stopped and an anguished scream echoed in Jemma's mind. Silence followed again. She turned to Mary and smiled.

"He's trapped at the bottom of the mine shaft," Jemma said and pointed at the depression.

"Serves him right," Mary replied. "Fucking creepy asshole. Let's get out of here." Mary turned to go and Jemma followed her.

You'll regret this! Elbert's voice commanded in Jemma's mind.

"I don't think so, Grandfather. You're exactly where you should be."

When I— the voice ended again in a tortured scream.

"Better than anything we could do to him," Jemma said and they headed back toward the mansion.

EPILOGUE

Alex stepped from the limousine and reviewed the few remaining bits of the Balsom estate that still stood. Two brick chimneys at either end of the building and a few skeletal burned timbers barely clinging together were all that remained of the once palatial estate.

Palatial by Tuggville standards, he thought as he smirked. He glanced at the dozen or so cars in the driveway, all sitting with their doors and trunks opened. Someone had rifled through the cars. He doubted local thieves would come this far. He wasn't even sure there was such a thing as local thieves left in Tuggville. Perhaps it was looters or maybe something else. He shrugged.

He walked along the exterior of the foundation, taking care to avoid areas that seemed precarious. He noted it was hard to discern what had been where by just looking at it even in the waning daylight, so it took a trip down memory lane for him to reconstruct the estate from memory. He glanced at where the different floors and rooms had been, remembered the gatherings, the rituals and the sacrifices in nearly every room. He'd spent his childhood here and was somewhat sad to see it reduced to such a state of destruction. But, all things came and went. Life and death, the natural cycle unless you were canny enough to make other arrangements.

He stopped at the rear of the estate and looked down into the smoking ruin. He stepped over the wall and held his hand up to the edges of the ceiling that were left.

"Circle is broken," Alex murmured. "Elbert, what have you done?"

He retraced the steps Mary had taken just a few days earlier. He examined the altar and couldn't find the old book anywhere. He kicked the altar and screamed in anger.

That was when Alex heard the whisper in his mind. Elbert called from somewhere in the growing darkness. The disturbance certainly wasn't a ghost, which would be a very surprising turn of events. Alex ascended the steps quickly. He turned to the two men waiting by the limousine and waved them forward. They ran to his side immediately. He pointed at them with a youthful hand that sharply contrasted his seventy years of age.

"Fetch flashlights and the GPS. We're going treasure hunting," he said and the men ran back to the limousine, fetched the items quickly from the trunk and returned to his side within minutes.

"Now follow me; I'm not sure how far we'll be traveling, but our quarry is incredibly important," Alex said as he held his hand up for quiet and then moved every time he heard Elbert's voice reach out to his mind. It took painstaking hours to traipse around the estate and through the forest before Alex and his companions finally reached the clearing.

Brother! Elbert's voice called out loudly to Alex's mind. *Dig me out!*

"Dear brother, what have you gotten yourself into?" Alex mused.

That bitch— Elbert's voice then screamed in Alex's mind. Alex frowned. It took several minutes before Elbert's voice returned in his head. *—trapped me in this mine shaft!*

"Well, this is an incredibly inefficient way of communicating. How about I dig you out of there?"

Yes! Elbert cried out. *This dying and resurrecting is driving me mad!*

"Patience, dear brother. It will take some equipment and logistics to get this going. I'm afraid you'll just have to put up with the cycle for a little while longer," Alex replied.

Alex turned to the two men. "Take measurements of the area, mark it with GPS, contact the geological department and coordinate the dig with them. You may need to return with some additional equipment to take measurements, but we need every hand on deck to unearth our prize at the bottom of that collapsed mine shaft. Confidential protocols, of course."

A month later, the area around the collapsed mine shaft had been transformed into a major drilling and digging operation. A path was cleared between the Balsom estate and through the forest to make way for heavy earthmoving equipment and all the supplies to build a shaft down to the buried brother.

Even with all the resources devoted to the dig, it still took months to erect the shaft and dig down before a naked, elderly man climbed out of the dirt. A basket was lowered; the man climbed into it and was brought to the surface.

Alex sat nearby at a picnic table arrayed with food. As the basket was raised, Alex dismissed most of the personnel with the exception of a few equipment operators that were kept at a sufficient distance where they couldn't overhear the ensuing conversation between the brothers.

One of the security men handed a robe to Elbert as he exited the basket. Elbert nodded at the man and put the robe on slowly. He hobbled over to the table with the assistance of the man. Elbert was mere skin and bones at this time and he fell onto the food and drink, consuming it greedily.

Every few minutes, Elbert would fall to the ground dead as his body died from the shock of consuming food and drink after so long. Minutes later, he would get back up from the ground, alive again and looking much better. He ran through this cycle a dozen times before he began to resemble his old self. Through it all, Alex silently watched and smiled enigmatically.

"I see the process works," Alex said as Elbert sat down at the table after a dozen rebirth cycles and slowly munched on a sandwich and some wine. "I haven't had a chance to test it myself."

"It isn't pleasant, but it's functional," Elbert replied. "Have you brought a decent set of clothes? This robe is nice, but I'd much prefer something suitable."

"In a moment," Alex said and leaned forward. "But first, tell me—where is she?"

"Where is who?" Elbert said as he drank his wine slowly.

His eyes darted over to the security guards.

"She who holds our master?"

Elbert filled the glass with more wine and drank it a bit more greedily.

"Jemma is in the wind," Elbert replied. "She can't have gotten far. She barely has any resources to her name."

"She is far more resourceful than you could imagine. Not to worry, my people are looking for her. I just wanted to know why you failed. You had one job," Alex said as he smiled, "and you failed at it spectacularly."

Elbert looked at the security guards again and then drank a full gulp of the wine. "You can't be serious," Elbert said. "She can't have come to any harm."

"I'll be the judge that," Alex said. "And then there's the matter of the book. It wasn't really your job to guard it, but I didn't foresee the destruction of the estate. Since the cataclysm destroyed the runes and sigils guarding it, I have to assume it was moved or destroyed by the incredibly powerful Lady Balsom."

"She was responsible for the destruction, yes," Elbert resumed his consumption of food and wine at a more leisurely pace. "I don't recall seeing her with the book."

"And where is the good Lady Balsom now?" Alex asked. He poured himself a glass of wine and swirled it around a bit. He gave it a subtle sniff and then sipped it briefly.

"Destroyed. Merged with Abigail somehow." Elbert set the glass down briefly and picked up a sandwich with both hands. He began to devour it noisily.

Alex stiffened. He looked back toward the house. Even

now there were sounds from the construction crew dismantling the estate while they continued to search through the wreckage. He scowled at his brother. "Abigail was here?" Alex asked.

Elbert gave him a wry smile in response.

"You put her in the basement, didn't you?" Alex asked.

"Well, of course I did. That's where I keep all my toys while I play with them," Elbert leaned forward with a grin. "I figured out how to put boils on one of them with that book! It was delightful. The other experiments didn't all go as well. I had some special plans for Abigail though—a little stroll down memory lane."

"Think," Alex stated. He gave Elbert a grim smile.

"What?"

"When you originally had your sick little tryst with a young Abigail Partridge, she was naïve, not yet formidable in the arts."

"Yes," Elbert grinned. "She was delightfully innocent before I introduced her to pain, humiliation and hate. What's your point?"

"What has she become since then?"

"An annoying thorn in my side, that's what," Elbert shouted. "Put up her little protection circles and damn runes. Couldn't get within fifty feet of her until good old Granny blew her house down."

"So, you brought an accomplished witch, a surviving relative of Lady Balsom, to the protected room where Lady Balsom's grimoire resides, unable to be moved by anything other than magical means which we never discovered. How do you think she was able to merge with Lady Balsom's incarnation, you moron?"

"Except for Granny herself, the Balsoms were all killed by my own hand," Elbert said as he stood up.

"She's not a Balsom, she's a Partridge. They're blood relatives. Cousins. How can you be so thick?"

"I don't care who she is—I can do what I want with whom I want!"

Alex stood up and walked up to Elbert who stood just a bit taller than his younger brother.

"You have near infinite resources. All you had to do was build another fucking dungeon for your stinking perversions," Alex spit the last two words in Elbert's face. "Instead, you've endangered us all. You've single-handedly lost the key to our future and the key to our destruction."

"It will be handled," Elbert said through gritted teeth.

"You've lost the vision of our new world," Alex said as he went back to his chair and sat down. He picked up his glass of wine.

"I don't need this repudiation by the likes of you." Elbert sat down in his own chair. He picked up his wine glass and took a drink. The glass trembled noticeably in his hand.

Alex smirked.

"You're free to leave," Elbert said and waved his hand dismissively.

"Oh, I think I'll be staying around for quite a while to clean up the mess you've made," Alex replied. "Meanwhile, you're of no further use to me."

Elbert stood up and slammed the glass down so hard on

the picnic table that it shattered in his grip, splashing his robe with wine and shards of glass. "I will not be spoken to in such a manner," Elbert fumed. "I'm the elder brother!"

"You're the weaker brother," Alex replied. "Always at the beck and call of your vices." Alex nodded at the security guards and they advanced on Elbert. He attempted to flee, but they grabbed him by the arms.

"Toss him back in the hole," Alex said as he stood up from the table. He grinned at Elbert. "It's really the only reason I brought you back up."

"No!" Elbert screamed. "You can't do this! I'm the elder!"

"Oh, fine," Alex said. "Let him keep the robe."

Alex watched as the security guards dragged Elbert back to the lip of the shaft and tossed him back down. Elbert's body crumpled as it hit the boards lining the shaft, his flesh catching on the random nails and screws jutting out from the surfaces. He hit the bottom of the shaft with a wet thud as parts of his body broke open on impact, his skull shattered into a dozen pieces spraying blood and brain matter on the walls of the shaft.

Alex walked to the edge of the shaft and looked down. Lights shining down the shaft illuminated his brother's destroyed body. It took nearly an hour, but eventually Elbert's bits and pieces of flesh rejoined each other and reformed.

"Fascinating," Alex murmured as he sipped his wine.

Elbert sat up in a bloody robe and shook his fist at his brother.

"Send that bucket down and let me out!" Elbert shouted.

"Oh, no, dear brother. I like you right there. It will be easy to find you if I need you."

"I'll climb back out of here and kill you!" Elbert screamed.

"Oh, good point," Alex said as he looked to the equipment operators standing by and waved them over. "Fill it back up with dirt and rocks. All the way to the top."

"No!" Elbert screamed. "You bastard!"

"Such eloquence under pressure," Alex said and walked away as the heavy equipment operators began to dump tons of earth of gravel into the shaft.